ANDERMATT COUNTY:

Two Parables

Pam Jones

APRIL GLOAMING

© 2017 by Pam Jones
illustrations © 2017 by Drew Holden

Publisher's Cataloging-in-Publication Data

Jones, Pam
    Andermatt county / by Pam Jones /
edited by Aaron Joel Lain, Ericka Suhl, & Lance Umenhofer /
designed by Drew Holden
    ISBN 978-0-9882061-5-1

1. Fiction 2. Fiction–21st Century I. Title

Library of Congress Control Number: 2017957480

by Pam Jones

edited by Aaron Joel Lain, Ericka Suhl,
& Lance Umenhofer

designed by Drew Holden

TO NATE RAGOLIA

Welcome to Andermatt County. Hill country. South-central Texas. The residents walk the terrain and feel the air as if in a haze of their own self-interest. The children live in a mystical void of wonder mixed with downtrodden hopes of their lives to come.

In YE SHALL BE AS GODS, meet Emmett Anhalt, a young, curious boy who lives with all women, none of them giving him the time of day, so he embarks on a walk through the brush and woods where he is introduced to the alluring ways of Rex Henry Burr—a serial killer. Emmett and Rex's journeys together are chronicled in this story, along with the lives and hopes and dreams of their victims and other residents of Andermatt County, each with his or her own personal quirks and downfalls.

In HAPPY BIRTHDAY, DEAR BITSY, we are introduced to the proverbial paradise of living in Andermatt County's social circles. Esther Fielding, or bitsy, is turning six years old, and her mother only wishes for her to replace her love for dead squirrels and rodents with a love for dolls and teatimes. But is she doing this solely for herself? Or is Esther already limpidly trudging down the right road?

"Kicking in the front door like the wild-eyed daughter of Cormac McCarthy, waving around a thirty-ot-six, with a single tear rolling down her face, Pam Jones grabs you by the collar and takes you to a Texas that you've never been to, but recognize immediately. Full of old ghosts and an underlying, melancholy sweetness that never wears out its welcome, the Andermatt County duology is a breath of fresh air…Out west, they say you've got to let horses run, and by the time you put this book down, that horse is long gone, and you're begging it to come back."

– Shaun Grulkowski, *author of Recontinuum and The Necronaut*

"Pam Jones' Andermatt County is a perfect gothic pairing written with precise and spectacular beauty. Cruel and delicate, these parables are fearless explorations of the mysterious nature of loneliness, grace and human connection. Jones has a style and grit that is all her own."

– Kelly Luce, *author of Pull Me Under*

YE SHALL BE AS GODS

"Creeping in from forests,
forms conjoin to assemble
one gargantuan black robed priest.
The townspeople sweep,
chant, light candles,

cradle pieces of warmth,
this one I will protect, that one, lost."

- Jennifer MacBain-Stephens, from "Pilgrimage,"
in *The Messenger is Already Dead*

MANTRA

"I think I'm an animal," Emmett said. He rolled in the bed in order to address the older man who lay beside him.

"Well," the older man said and nodded against the pillow they shared; he looked very sage, putting Emmett at ease. "That's what you are, then. Does that bother you?"

Emmett puzzled. He listened for a beat to the radio, tuned to the blues and jazz station from Austin: Chet Baker, "I Fall in Love Too Easily." He let his eyes adjust to the blue dark of the bedroom. The house was theirs, just about everything in it, save for the clutter of things on the bureau top. Two hair ribbons (one green, one white), a blue

1

silk hydrangea blossom, a pink lipstick, a penny, a pillbox the size of your palm that rattled when you handled it. The older man had told him, "Just because we have those things in our house doesn't mean they belong to us. And you gotta know that."

On the radio, Chet Baker faded out, and the older man reached to change the station, classical, a soprano whose voice pierced the back of Emmett's throat.

> "...Mentre del mare nel profondo seno
> Sta la tempesta ascosa..."

Emmett heaved himself out of the bed and went to kneel at the foot of the bureau. He pawed until he had the pillbox in hand, its contents careening from one end to the other with a hollow spray, like rice in a rain stick. He lifted the lid. Inside, relics: the real treasure: thirty or so tiny and white teeth. Emmett looked with reverence, but did not remove a single one.

Now the old man said again, "Does that bother you?"

Then Emmett uttered his oft-used phrase, "I don't know."

MATINS

It had been a pain whenever he answered anything with *I don't know*. His mother would bark at him, ask him if he knew anything at all.

Well, what DO you know? Mr. Selmon bellowed for his audience, fifteen-year-olds who liked dunces.

Ninth grade was as far as Emmett had gone in school, and that was enough for him.

One day, he just did not go.

There was Emmett, not so much playing hooky as following a smoky train of thought, going the opposite side of the street than the one he usually went to school, going along the road that ran beside the Canadian River until he got to its sandy edge. And he thought he knew what called him there.

The Standing Rock, which rose like the twist of a great tree trunk from the middle of the water, was going to disappear. In a few days, some mysterious collection of workers, all big talk and concrete, were coming to dam the river. Eufaula Lake, they would call it, after the town. His mother had read it aloud from the paper that morning. At the time Emmett thought she said they were going to *damn the river*. Fire, brimstone, all that.

At the river's shore he got comfortable. He slipped out of his shoes, knotted his socks and balled them in his hip pocket. His mother was not there to shout at him, and so he removed his school corduroys, his shirt. As it grew warmer, his hair paled from mousy brown to white. He was long, lean—his skin crosshatched with tiny scars. Clothes were a burden, one more layer of skin than he felt he needed. He was never cold, and he often paired colors incorrectly, green with blue or brown with black. What little scrapes he got in his nudity he took without flinching. He spent his time outdoors this way.

He piled his clothes on a bench, anchored them with his schoolbooks. Then he dug a pit into the sand and defecated, and watched, with eyes that caught the world around him in quick, sharp edges, for anyone who might be coming.

The rock looked more or less like what had come out of him. He buried his mess quickly, so that no one would know he had been there.

Emmett spent the day at the lake, and thus far he'd not seen a soul. He slept when he needed it. When hungry, he swiped crappies from the water and ate them with his hands. He submerged himself in the green of the river and listened to his pulse drumming one, two, three, four, five, to one hundred, before he burst to the surface. On the shore he draped the shirt, warm flannel, over his shoulders like a cape and read one of the books that weighed the rest of his clothes. *What Maisie Knew*.

"Poor kiddo," he said aloud of the title's heroine. These were the first words he'd spoken in hours. When he wasn't outdoors, he was reading. He learned things about people from books that he couldn't in face-to-face circumstances. People never came out and exposed themselves. He didn't know what he would do without books; very likely, he would not see himself, and his fellow man would not see him. And even if he got to a point at which he had read every novel, every history, every diary in every library, he would never shake the notion of the schism between what people felt and what he was supposed to feel for them. They hurt, but he did not. They wept, but he could not.

Simple as that.

That must have been roughly the time the older man appeared. He looked to be taking pictures of the land around them, for he stood behind what seemed to be an old-fashioned camera—boxy, atop a tripod. He was too far away to tell.

When the lens of this device veered Emmett's way, Emmett himself could think of nothing better to do than to sit and stare.

In school, many years ago when he was just starting out and when he was too young to receive any serious punishment, a girl in a brown dress had called him a spastic. His first reaction was to do nothing. He would sit and stare and, hopefully, she would lose her wind and walk away. The girl was made of stronger stuff. *Spastic spastic, SPAZ SPAZ SPAAAAZ*, her lips vibrating around the word. Her teeth were tiny and white and square. Finally, she came up and pushed him, a soft poke to the shoulder, really. And he bit her bottom lip. It hung like a slice of ham from her mouth. She shrieked, and Emmett's mother, chilled, then paid for the girl's stitches. Word must have gotten out about what he had done, because after that, people let him be.

And now there was a camera on him.

He hadn't tried to cover himself. He had said, "Don't take my picture."

The older man coughed and told him that he was not taking pictures. "I'm a land surveyor. This is a theodolite."

"What do you do with it?"

"You measure angles. Oughtn't you s'posed to be at school?"

"I didn't go."

"I see that." He looked to be fifty, maybe sixty, and a cigarette perked from the corner of his lip. Emmett's mother had told him to look at his Aunt Jennie: "She smokes like a chimney. Guess how old she is. Well, she's forty. And it's because she smokes like a chimney she looks eighty." If this was true, the man could have been Emmett's own age, and that was not a man just yet. He wore men's clothes, sure enough, hard boots and a khaki windbreaker, a flat-topped cap of the sort you might wear on a golf course.

The man asked Emmett's name.

Emmett told him. He thought of giving him a throwaway name, Barabbas or Hercules, but nothing leapt to mind.

"That a family name?" the man asked, shifting the cap on his head. He plucked the cigarette from his mouth to ash it.

"No. I don't know anyone by that name in my family. I'm the only fellow."

The man craned his head back, nonplussed. "The only one?"

"Me, my mother. Aunts, too, but neither of them married."

Aunt Jewel had what she called a "beau." Sometimes she lived with him, sometimes she came storming back to Emmett's mother's house and told him to "Keep out of my damn way. Have you nothing else to do but look at me and make my skin crawl?" She read auras and claimed Emmett brought bad mojo: "Anyone who looks at someone and has nothing to say to them—it's unnatural." His Aunt Jennie was a suicide, but she wasn't dead. She'd jumped off the roof of her apartment house last April and landed in the street: fractured backbone, shattered right femur, kidney trauma, and sourness in her gut. Emmett's mother made up the TV room for her, and she lay on the couch, ashing cigarettes into her water glass and watching *What's My Line?* She had difficulty moving her right side and liked Emmett to be the one who dressed and bathed her. "No man's going to touch me again," she would tell him. "But you'll do."

The older man asked, "Don't you get lonesome? Being the only fellow?"

"I don't know." Emmett had long ago reasoned that there was the world and there was him, and thus all would remain divided. It wasn't something he thought he ought to feel one way or the other about.

"What say you come along with me?"

Emmett blushed: "Come along to where?"

"Home," the older man said. "With me."

"You live around here?"

"No."

"Then where do you live?" Emmett had been as far as Tahlequah, where the traffic signs were written in English and in scrolling Cherokee letters. He was seven at the time and slept for much of the trip. He thought they went up to Canada, through Alaska, and were now in Russia. A few hundred miles was international travel.

"Andermatt." The older man flicked his cigarette into the grit and smeared it with the toe of his boot. "County seat of Andermatt County."

"Where's that?"

"Texas, in the hill country. Real pretty down there. Bluebonnet season now."

LAUDS

Emmett wanted to ask how it came to be that the man was surveying land up here and not down there, but he kept quiet. He reasoned that if he were to go with this man to Andermatt County, he would never have to go to school again. Perhaps he would never have to dress again, either, as the man did not appear unnerved by Emmett's nudity.

Fleetingly, he reasoned that his mother might wonder where he was, or one of his aunts. He did not see any reason why they would not be relieved at his vanishing; it was a small house. These two years past, he was forced to give up his bedroom for one of the aunts and bunk with his mother. They slept tops and tails in her bed, and in the night she would kick. She smelled of Max Factor and onions.

He would never have to smell her again.

He could smell this man from here, a thousand odors that recalled bacon, or any sort of meat to be fried, and the bitterness of the cigarettes layered upon the man's clothes. Emmett had always loved the smell of cigarettes.

"Ought I to get dressed?" Emmett asked. Grit had collected between his legs.

The man nodded, slow, as though he'd had to think on it, weigh the pros and cons. "Yes, you ought to." The man knelt and collapsed the tripod on which the theodolite stood. "For now. It's an eight-hour or so drive back to the hill country. When we get there, you can let loose."

"May I bring my books?" Emmett's school-books, his required reading for this semester's English, jittered with a passing breeze.

"If you want. I have quite a library at my place. Homer, Shakespeare, all that. The scriptures being my favorite."

"You're faithful?"

"No, not as such. But it helps to keep in practice."

Emmett dressed and followed him.

Behind him, through the rear window of a '49 Chevrolet pickup the color of a raw heart, he watched the Standing Rock shrink, smaller and smaller, until it became a crumb on the flat horizon. In another hour, the sun would set, and in that hour they would cross the state line.

ST. ANTHONY

In that hour, his mother would begin paring fat from pork chops. Aunt Jewel, peeling carrots, would peer between the curtains at the gloaming. "Well," she would say, "it's finally happened."

"What's that?" his mother would ask.

"He's flown the coop. Your boy."

"How do you know that?"

"Trust me. He's gone. I feel lighter between my shoulder blades. It means he's not looking at me."

"What?"

"Just trust me, hon. He's gone."

His mother would never admit to herself that the following sigh was one of relief. The beagle sat, fat and pitiful, at her feet and emitted piggy grunts. The old thing drooled and stank, but you could always guess what she wanted when she looked at you. "Give me those scrapings when you're through," Emmett's mother said to Aunt Jewel, and added them to the plate of pork trimmings.

The beagle, delighted, bent and ate, and she hardly chewed to get it all down.

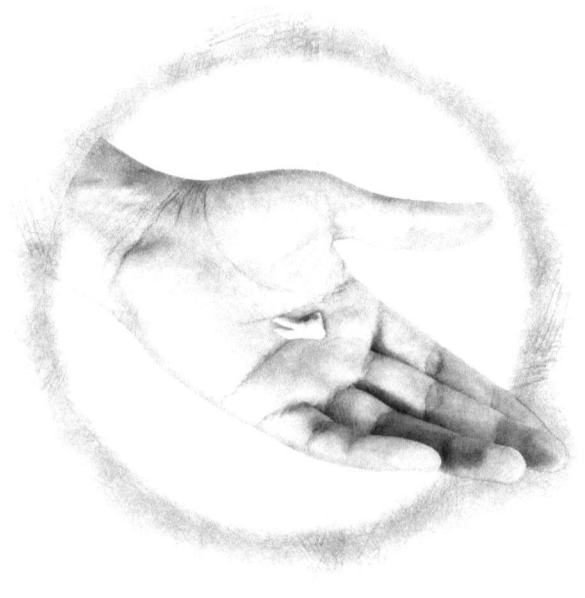

PRIME

Time passed, and the land's curves flattened and remained that way for so long that Emmett wondered if the rest of the country was going to be like this. Plano, Dallas, Killeen, Johnson City. But, little by little, the road met some resistance as they reached the hills. There were trees, too, shrubby ones and spindly ones with branches like witches' paws, twisting out of the craterous ground. The older man mentioned that this part of the country had once been at the bottom of an ocean.

A sign, carved from cedar and painted in the bright, fancy Dutch style, read, "Wilkommen!" And beneath that, in larger letters, "Welcome to Andermatt County!" And beneath that, a list of all

its incorporated villages: "Home to Andermatt, El
Velo, Sola, Himmel Creek."

Emmett did not volunteer much about himself, and neither did the older man, save to inform
Emmett that his name was Rex Henry. "Rex Henry
Burr," the older man said, his hands firmly gripping the wheel at ten and two. "My family wanted
nobility in it, but I doubt there was any to be had."

Emmett eyed the constant setting beyond
the window: the long, thin line that separated
the highway from the grass and the mud. Every
now and then, the sameness was interrupted by a
bunch of flowers, a pile of rag dolls, pairs of shoes
arrayed along the edge of the road, a cross hewn
out of wood and painted purple. When Rex Henry
slowed to the speed limit, Emmett could see a wavering procession moving up the edge of the road.
At first, all he could make out were sparks, shards
of light that were there and then not, moving up
the road as though on an assembly line. When they
drove up a bit farther, faces emerged in the glow
of these sparks, which were the flames from small
candles. Emmett turned in his seat; one by one
each of these marchers approached the roadside
trinkets, the dolls, the shoes, the cross, to lay their
candles, to bow their heads.

"What're they doing?" Emmett asked.

"Girl gone missing." Rex Henry shifted in the

captain's seat and plucked the knob for the radio. Chet Baker sings *"I fall in love too easily..."*

"Is she dead?"

"I don't think so. Just missing."

"All that, and she isn't deceased?" Emmett liked to use the better words from his vocabulary when the moment warranted.

Rex Henry pursed his lips. "I believe they've given up. That's why the parade."

Outside, up the highway, the marchers began a hymn. Their voices, caught in the air, gathered and wafted like smoke in all directions.

> *"Art thou weary, art thou languid*
>
> *Art thou sore distressed?"*

Rex Henry let his eyes drift away from the procession, its participants reduced in the dark to the flickering of their candles. When he drove, his posture became gnomish, his head retreating between his shoulders so that he peered over the top of the steering wheel. "We ought to be near Andermatt by eight or so."

"Okay."

"You like movies?"

Emmett thought. "I don't know. I suppose so."

23

The last film he had seen was *Meet Me in St. Louis*, on the Tahlequah trip, in that smaller life. His mother and his Aunt Jewel had cried during that picture, sobbing that it was wonderful. It hadn't seemed at the time that you ought to enjoy a thing if it made you cry. So far, in his books, he had yet to read of anyone weeping for joy. It seemed outside the natural order of what pleasure was meant to be. And this was a feeling that escaped him still, for surely there were things he liked that others might find disagreeable. It was all very murky.

"Well, we'll go see the stars," Rex Henry said. "My treat."

"Okay."

The line of sparks continued, at least a mile more down the highway. The marchers farther on echoed the first lines of "Art Thou Weary?" Not a one of them had a trained voice, and the hymn was better for its roughness. It made Emmett shiver; he bit his forefinger to contain it.

"How long is she gone for?" he murmured, like someone in church.

Rex Henry swallowed. And he smiled. "Only a few weeks."

"Seems like they gave up on her quick enough."

"Yes."

"Everyone must've liked her a lot."

Rex Henry reached to snuff the radio, inviting the ghost of the hymn to slip between the window cracks and through the radiator. Finally, Rex Henry said, "I don't know about that."

Emmett nodded, a bit fuzzily. He'd been rooting in the wastebasket bolted to the passenger-side door. With reverence and a steady hand, as though he were handling artifacts at a museum, Emmett lifted each item to his eye and put it back without a sound. A pencil. A hydrangea blossom, blue and made of something like silk. A Canadian penny. A note on lined paper, folded and tucked into a square that read: "Would you rather A) Lose your virginity to the man of your dreams, but in front of an audience? B) Have the best first time, but never Do It again? C) Be hot and bothered 24/7, but only for Mr. Powell?" A finger ring set with a dot of amethyst, a birthstone.

And the last token.

Emmett held it between thumb and forefinger, a pearl.

A tooth.

"It's pretty," he whispered.

It was sharp and milky blue, spotless, incorruptible. It would survive the elements, the years.

Emmett put it in his shirt pocket.

Rex Henry nodded, for although no permission had been asked, it had been accepted. Of course, Emmett could keep it.

They reveled in it, the way you do when you have found, at last, your Other. That instant when you know, for sure, that there is not only one of you, and that another will, one day, make the recognition. The feeling was golden. A life could be made for Emmett and Rex Henry.

Miles passed, three or four, and the line of mourners and their candles dwindled and disappeared. The echo of the hymn drifted into the air, a single note rising and wafting away, then becoming swallowed by highway babble. The last line stuck with them, *"...Saints, apostles, prophets, martyrs/Answer, Yes!"* They let it burrow and make them its host for the miles that came, so much so that Emmett switched off the radio to let the silence make the words clearer. He fingered the tooth in his breast pocket, not believing it now belonged to him. He felt that a great bit of something like luck or a blessing had been given him; something in him had shifted.

Rex Henry waited until they reached the city limits of El Velo to ask if Emmett was hungry.

Emmett nodded. He'd been going through the wastebasket a second time. An eraser. A hair ribbon. A piece of chewing gum, still mint-flavored, Emmett found when he put it in his mouth.

Rex Henry said, "I don't know if she was liked, but she was a good girl. Of that I am certain. No one would have known it, otherwise. Isn't that sad?"

Emmett agreed, it was sad.

"Think what might have happened if this had never come to her. She might have just vanished."

Emmett chewed and nodded.

"She's got friends now, as you saw back there. Lots of them."

Emmett turned to look, though they were a long way now from the procession. He half-expected, even this far away, to see the tail end of the mourners' parade, one more flickering candle. He dug out the note again, opened it. A title was scrawled across the top, "PERSONAL-ITY TEST…FOR YOUR EYES ONLY!!!" He scanned it. Mr. Powell must be a fusty old teacher. The test itself was unmarked.

Emmett was familiar with these things, made out for, it seemed, the low bird on the pecking order, the one in class who sat, did not talk, did not laugh or cry. The rock you may squeeze blood from, if only you knew how to crack it. Emmett was never given any of these tests himself; no one could crack him, and no one dared to try. He had always been one of the hands that passed the note, back, back, back, to the rear of the class where the good girls always sat. Was it the same all the world over? Did good girls everywhere sit in the back? At any rate, he'd gotten a peek at one or two questionnaires. One had read, "How Stacked Are Yoo-Hoo?," the Os in *Yoo-Hoo* dotted in the middle to make breasts. The girl who got them (a prim little thing with a virtue name, like Anne Faith or Anne Truth) let her eye flick over the words, and then, po-faced, she would put it away.

Was it meant to be funny?

He recounted the story for Rex Henry, whom he felt ought to know a thing or two.

Rex Henry said, "I'll bet you they don't know the half of what they're talking about. To them, it's the forbidden fruit. They don't know what it's all about, what it tastes like, so they'll slime it up to make it into something they can understand."

"What about the good girl? Does she know what it's all about?"

Rex Henry paused, slowed to the speed limit, for they were entering the center of town. Lights, pink and green, advertising hamburgers and ice cream. Then he intoned, "I think so. I think she does. Or at least, she can imagine it. She can—she can sympathize. That's what makes her blush. To her, it's a serious affair."

"Is that good?"

"I would say so."

"Like me getting unclothed wherever?"

"Yes. Just like that. Now, The Carnelian Café and Rock Shop. The Rock Shop's closed, but we can still get a bite in the café part. How's that sound?"

Emmett nodded.

He wanted to know what made the difference between a thing that was quiet and a thing that was ordinary.

MEMORIAL CRUMB

Renata Ansky said, "Please," right until the very end.

She was a good girl, though she sat square in the middle of the class, not in the back.

What did she do on her own time? What did she like? Everyone wondered, now that she was gone. It was, indeed, a full assumption, for she had vanished without a trace, both body and soul.

Well, she liked blue hydrangeas, and mint-flavored gum, and strawberry shortcake, and cats, and Tchaikovsky, and Emily Dickinson. This ought to form a fair equation to what Renata Ansky was all about.

What makes the difference between a thing that is quiet and a thing that is ordinary?

On that last day, Renata sat in the square middle of her English class, and she wanted nothing more than to be invisible. Which was not to say that she did not want anyone to notice her for the right reasons. She was fourteen and love was undiscovered territory. Not in the romantic sense, exactly; it seemed to be the sort of thing that could be passed on, ought to be passed on, from one person to another, in the manner of contagion. And yet everyone, herself included, seemed to have moments of immunity. For instance, she had not been kind to that girl in the lunchroom, the one who wept and wept, openly, messily, without regard for the whispers, the faces pulled to ask, "What's her problem? What's she blubbering for?" Public crying, Renata found, cast a chill within a room, even on a hot day, as that day had been.

It had made Renata sick to look at the girl. And so, she'd eaten her lunch, pretended that the girl was not there, at the very end of her own table. Here was one universe, Renata's, and there was the girl's, her misery eons away.

"It shouldn't be so hard," she thought, and caught someone to her left looking at her, and then to her right. Then in front, then in back.

She had spoken aloud, enough for those

around her to take notice, if not the teacher. Mr. Powell was reading loudly from a heavy tome, a collection of poetry and some psalms. His voice was caught somewhere between his throat and his nose, and he quacked through the verses.

"If I shouldn't be alive

When the robins come

Give the one in red cravat

A memorial crumb…"

Would Renata still love Dickinson if Dickinson quacked? It was nasty to think of herself, Renata Ansky, tittering away and losing the words to a woman who quacked.

She played with the little appliqué on her sweater, a blue hydrangea that was coming loose. Sure enough, a petal (viscose, not silk) fell to her desk. There was a bit of paper there that hadn't been before, folded tightly into a football. Now she understood the four faces. All of them, the ones to her left and right, the ones in front and in back, were ballooned and pink with swallowed laughter.

What did they call Renata Ansky?

Goody-goody.

Goody-two-shoes.

Space cadet.

Spaz.

Tighty-whitey.

She didn't even curse. It was common knowledge. She sometimes wished she never told Kay Wiley (the girl on her left) that she did not hate. Then, Kay Wiley had told Glenda Stahl (the girl on Renata's right), who told Maxine Bickler (the girl who sat behind Renata), who told Willie Palacky (the girl who sat in front). "And neither should you," Renata recalled herself saying, like a little tighty-whitey. In her imagination, she'd been quacking. "And it shouldn't be so hard. You ought to know that." Suddenly, Renata Ansky was cringing at her own sanctimony.

Who did she think she was?

She opened the Personality Test. It was one of those that determined if you were a Hot Mama or a Cold Fish depending on how many questions you answered A, B, or C. They knew it would make her go red in the face, red as a strawberry. They'd seen that before.

Would you rather be hot and bothered 24/7, but only for Mr. Powell?

If I shouldn't be alive...

Willie Palacky, twisting herself so tightly around in her seat she could barely breathe, glanced first at the test, then at Renata—though never at her eyes. None of them could ever look directly at her, Renata had long ago learned. Kay looked at her nose. Glenda looked at her fingers. Maxine looked at her hair, a dark mane unpinned and unbraided. Willie looked at her mouth. Renata had a daydream in which these pieces of herself, unattached, chased and then snatched these girls, holding them fast. They shrieked, they squirmed, they turned their faces away. *You look at me*, Renata would bellow. *Look at me.*

Like the girl in the lunchroom? Renata heard herself murmur, somewhere far at the back of her mind, inaudible, for she did not want to hear it. *You stuffed down chop suey like your life depended on it, and you couldn't even look at her.*

The weeping girl had not been in school today. Renata was spared that. She blinked, shook her head. Absently, she dropped the piece of gum she'd been chewing into the Personality Test. Vaguely, she saw Willie Palacky huff and turn around. What was the girl's name? What had she looked like? Renata kneaded the edge of the test paper and thought. Brownish hair, maybe reddish. Shortish. Was she skinny, round, just right? Did the girl wear glasses? How old was she? What did her voice sound like? Had someone died? A grandmother? A pet? Was the girl sick? Was she lonely, weary, languid? Did her name start with an E?

"Let's talk about the crumbs," Mr. Powell

35

quacked. "*Memorial* crumbs. Significance?"

Elana? Elaine?

"Are they tokens? What do we do when we visit a cemetery? Miss Palacky?"

Emma?

"I leave bluebonnets when I visit my grand-dad's grave. The crumbs are a little like that, I guess."

Was it Emma? Renata felt far away now. Was it Emma?

Mr. Powell began another poem.

> *"I heard a Fly buzz—when I died—*
>
> *The Stillness in the Room—"*

And like that. Of course. Like the final trickle that breaks the dyke, Renata knew everything about the weeping girl.

She glanced over her shoulder, through Maxine Bickler's head, to the last row of desks. The ones who never talked at all sat there, backed up against the bookcase. No one really knew what they looked like, save for their clothes: a red sweater, a plaid skirt. These were the truly invisible, even amongst themselves.

Thankfully, Philip D. Andermatt High School was a small one, and everyone knew everyone else since the first grade. If you didn't immediately

36

know faces, you knew names. You knew where people sat. Renata went down the row with her eyes, and she began to *see to see*, as Dickinson said. Here was Mike Witte, who was ambidextrous. Next to him, Alma Flores, who always fed the stray cats outside the lunchroom. And next to her, an empty chair, where Emily Kitchen sat.

"Emily Kitchen," Renata whispered, and began to mine her brain's strata of things she didn't know she knew.

Emily Kitchen was Renata's age, fourteen. Their birthdays were a day apart, though no one knew it. The Kitchen family were Jehovah's Witnesses, and did not celebrate the usual paganism of Christmas, Easter, and birthdays. Emily liked Indian paintbrushes, and De La Rosa peanut candy, and apple pie, and frogs, and Edith Piaf, and Emily Dickinson.

That was something.

Renata planned it out before the end of class: She would go to Emily's house.

She did not know exactly where the Kitchens lived in Andermatt, but she did know that hers and Emily's fathers worked together at the post office. In that hidden strata, she unearthed a memory of someone saying (Mother? Mrs. Glau next door?) that the Kitchens did not have a car, and that Mr. Kitchen walked anywhere he needed to go. Might he live close enough to the post office for that? If so, finding Emily would be easier than Renata thought.

The bell rang.

From the steps of Philip D. Andermatt High School, you saw the panorama of the town, for anything anyone needed could be found on the Main Street. Here was the general store, and Popham's Grocery, and the Laundromat, and the Masonic Lodge where Renata's father went to his meetings every week, and Dear Liza's Café, and the Sweet Home Baptist Church, and the library, and, at last, at the end of the road just before Main Street turned into the greater highway, the post office. Up and down the highway were little houses, some crowded against the lip of the road and anchored there, it seemed, by chain-link fences, others set far back in the thicket of cedar shrubs so that they were barely visible.

It was fair to guess that the Kitchens lived in one of these houses.

Renata stopped first into the general store. There were no miniature fruit pies, but there was candy. She filled a paper bag with De La Rosa, careful not to crush any of them, and asked Vera at the register to tie it with that little piece of green ribbon.

"It's for doing hair with," Vera said.

Renata told her that this was a gift for some-one who needed cheer, and who might get a kick out of it if it had a bit of fancy.

"Well, aren't you sweet," Vera said, and made a pretty bow around the twisted end of the bag, even flared the paper edges up so that it had the look of a blossom. "One bit of fancy. There you go. Anything else you need today, babe?"

"Some Wrigley's Doublemint, if you have it. I didn't see any on the shelves."

"Well, we did run out. But I can spare some of what I got here…" Vera ducked under the counter and rooted through her handbag. "One pack of Doublemint, no charge."

"Oh, not all of it—"

"Well, hand me back a piece and we'll be even."

Outside, it was bluebonnet season, Indian paintbrush season. All along the road, every bit of spare grass was starred pink and indigo. Renata blew minty bubbles and dipped now and then, gathering flowers until she had an impressive bouquet; she passed the Baptist church, the library, trailing petals. In the post office window she rip-pled like a little freewheeling bride.

She set the bouquet on the counter.

"Now, look at this! Flowers for me?" Her

father patted his neck with a hankie and smiled.

Renata plucked a few bluebonnets from the bouquet for him and, as quickly as she could, keeping her voice low, she relayed her quest for him. The weeping girl, the candy, everything.

"People're going to think you're in love, bringing candy and flowers." Her father murmured this, his tone cryptic, perhaps unearthing something in his daughter before Renata could in herself. Renata could love anyone, he knew, for she saw to see. There had been that boy next door, and then that girl in her civics class. But, as much as he hated to do it, he would have to rein her in; you could take love too far, especially when you were young. "Just mind how that's going to look."

Renata couldn't think why that would matter. She told him not to be a fool. At the moment she was here on business, and she got to it. "Would you know where the Kitchens live, Pop?"

He thought. "They're a ways from town."

"But Mr. Kitchen walks to work, doesn't he?"

"That man can walk the Bataan Death March plus an extra mile. Why don't you wait 'til the end of the day and I can drop you there?"

Renata sighed. There were shards of pink and orange caught in her dark hair, petals already loosening from the bouquet. She was a patient girl, but she was not one to wait.

Her father knew that about her, too.

"Okay," he said finally. "With any luck, Karl Kitchen may well catch up with you halfway. Here's how you get there…"

And she walked. She went up the Main Street and on and on, where the road curved and wound around the steeper hills. It was a straight shot, her father said; the Kitchen house was one of those close up to the road, the little white brick one— the only white brick one, for all the others on the highway were built from limestone.

As Renata pressed on, the dust and distress around her brain cleared, layer by layer. She began to remember more about Emily Kitchen, more than her likes. Before setting out, Renata thought she would never quite remember Emily Kitchen's face because, well, who did? She figured she would know her when she saw her. But here, now, little fragments recalled themselves. Emily Kitchen had auburn hair, very long hair that she kept pinned to the crown of her head; here was a memory of Emily unraveling it after P.E., someone remarking that she ought to leave it down, it was so pretty. And grey eyes, no glasses. Pigeon toed, teeth like a rabbit's, a button nose dotted with freckles. A natural expression of dolorousness.

The first order of business, Renata decided,

was to make Emily Kitchen smile.

Time passed, and cars did, too. A souped Model T, black with a spray of flames. A grey Cadillac, trailing saxophone from its radio. A maroon Chevrolet pickup that made a turn onto a ranch road just ahead of her.

The sky pinked, then reddened, then purpled. It would not be dark enough yet for any motorists to turn on their headlights. Her throat burned, her mouth dry and gummy. Her eyelids grew heavy. She did little things to keep her mind turning, rehearsing what she might say to Emily Kitchen when she got to her house, *I was just around. I heard you were sick and thought I'd stop by.* When she tired of that, she counted the steps she took, *One hundred-and-six, one-hundred-and-seven, two-hundred, two-hundred-and-twelve,* or she would sing the little nonsense songs her father taught her, "Mairzy Doats and Dozy Doats," "I Go With the Garbage Man's Daughter." The flowers in her hand began to sag. Once or twice she thought she might stop somewhere, hunker down against a fencepost and rest her bones, just for a while, before setting off again.

But Renata was not one to wait. So she kept going.

She thought, at first, of Emily Kitchen and what her smile might be like, though it was difficult now to hold onto anything. Everything shifted, and no matter how often she swallowed, she could not be quenched. Her head drooped; her imagination spiked with visions of pilgrims in battered shoes and empty canteens, leaning on staffs as they made their way to the Holy Land. How many had dropped along the way, of thirst, exhaustion?

Had they known they would never make it?

Time passed, and cars did, too. Someone she knew in a blue Edsel slowed enough to wave at Renata. She squinted to see who the person might be, and if it was she they were waving at.

Then what happened? She had turned. She had turned and she had dropped the paper bag of De La Rosa candy, and heard them crush. She had watched as the world seemed to fall away.

A woman's voice. The odor of emission, then a man whose speech Renata felt somewhere between her shoulders and the base of her neck. It was not so much talking as a thick vibration. "She's all right. She's all right. She was headed up to my cousin's place, anyway. Yes, he's not far—"

She might have heard the trickling of a stream, the rustle and snuff of a white-tail deer, perhaps a boar.

She'd thought for sure she'd been alone all this time.

Had she been spotted, as a vulture spots a wounded faun, from behind the windows of the café, the Baptist church? And then tracked?

She would spend her final moments, scattered as they were, piecing this together.

Really, it would be hours.

"Please—" Renata felt as though she'd been saying this many, many times to deaf ears. Who had she been saying this to? To Emily Kitchen? To God? "Please—"

Vibrations slowly reconfigured themselves into words. "You're all right. You're all right." The woman in the blue Edsel was gone and they were alone.

Time passed, hours as minutes.

Renata came to, bit by bit. Here were the cedar shrubs, and there at eye-level was a cactus with its little buds of pears. Here were fragments of her bouquet, shards of pink and green that were bound now by Vera's fancy green ribbon. They lay at her feet, like a token left at a shrine. She could not have said whether she was upright or lying down, though she understood that something restrained her in this position.

Here was the world as Renata Ansky knew it, but altered and very curious. She noticed this when she noticed her shoes, beside the bouquet: they were both at her feet, but she had to look up to see them. She had just emerged from a dream in which she had been flying. Well, this was not wholly correct, not flying like a bird or Peter Pan. She had lifted one foot and then the other and webbed her arms and legs until she went up and up, the way she did when she swam from the bottom of the Andermatt Community Pool. She faded out; perhaps she had taken this piece of the dream with her into the waking life, and could swim in the air whenever she wanted.

Then she surfaced.

Where was the road?

There were trees and cacti, but no road. She meant to ask this to the man just above her. He was an unfortunate looking soul, with his eyes where his chin ought to be and his lips so close to his forehead. *Excuse me, mister, could you maybe tell me where…*

The man nodded, pulled at the ends of her hair, and wiped his hands with a towel, very, very reverently. "You're all right," he kept saying, "you're all right."

"Please—" The ends of her long, dark hair wafted against the ground, disturbing the surface rubble.

And here, Rex Henry Burr stepped back, back, back, to admire his work. He put his tools in his

45

pocket, mopped his brow. He eased himself against the side of the Chevrolet pickup the color of a raw heart, and looked, tried to imagine what he might make of this picture, this scene, if he were not its creator. It might be prideful, but he liked to compare these scenes to the work of an Old Master, a Carrivaggio, a Gentileschi, putting all the meat of humankind in its full and horrific glory. *O death, where is thy sting?*

Here was a girl, a maiden, suspended from her feet by electric cables, the branch of the cedar taking just so much of her weight. When she moved she bounced, but cedar was flexible. Here was her body, this precious vessel that leaked and leaked, a single laceration that traced her small breasts and intersected at her collar. Her hands drifted over the ground; if you squinted, she looked as though she were doing a handstand. Her hair wild. Her nudity, her girlhood unleashed but unmarred.

What did Rex Henry see? Symmetry, as much as he could hope for. There was serenity, too, acceptance of this fact of giving and taking away; you could see it in the maiden's face, that little ghost of a smile around her eyes. This is not to say that the girl wanted to die, far from it. Very likely, you could infer that it was her reflection on her good life and her joy at the one that was to come. She had been a lovely girl in life, all that wildness in her reined in and reined in, until now. You are never so much yourself in life as you are in death. He realized this when his father passed; the man died with a smile on his face.

Rex Henry remembered what to do from his hunting days, before his eyesight started to go. He'd sold his firearms and his spare ammunition, but kept his field dressing things. He wore thick glasses now, big bifocals that gave him a perpetual bug-eyed look. He was surprised he had seen her from his place in the post office line. He had come only for stamps, the new ones depicting state birds, and there she was. He saw what kind of stuff she was made of, just as easily as though she had turned around and told him.

"Please—" Her lips were red, then blue. Her breasts dripping so that they resembled nothing so much as candied apples. She had been muttering something else for a while, something that sounded like, "See she, see she, see she."

"What's that?" Rex Henry knelt, putting his ear close to her lips. "Say again?"

Renata Ansky tried. "See she—"

"See she? See she what? Who?"

"See she—see sheee—"

Rex Henry sifted through his brain. She? A name came to mind, Emily Kitchen. *Do you know where the Kitchens live, Pop?* Renata had said. He knew the Kitchens well, he and Mrs. Kitchen were members of the Great Books Club at the library. They lived in El Velo, Emily would be about this girl's age in school. Long red hair, small. She was a fretful little thing, he recalled, at the whim of funny moods. She did not eat meat. It was said that a rainy day could break her; she made people nervous and her cross to bear was that she knew it.

Renata croaked, "See she." Then, "Candy." Then, "Emily."

Rex Henry pawed his pocket. He'd lifted a few pieces of De La Rosa from Renata's bag when he whisked her away, left the rest. To his knowledge, the bag was still there, just where the boundaries of Andermatt and El Velo touched.

Candy and flowers, for love. Rex Henry couldn't say no to that. It was as though she had blessed him.

He nodded and drew a line across her throat. He sat and counted the minute it took to extinguish Renata Ansky's underground fire. He murmured, "What a piece of work is man," and forgot the rest. He cut her down and rendered her, piece by piece, and piled her neatly with brush and dry grass. Before lighting her funeral pyre, it came back to him, and he wondered at how he could have lost it. She burned and he intoned, "*What a piece of work is a man! How noble in reason! How infinite in faculty! In form, in moving, how express and admirable. In action, how like an angel! In apprehension, how like a god! The beauty of the world! The paragon of animals!'"*

He finished and reached into the flames. It was difficult to tell now which pieces of her were which, for everything collided together to become ash. But he knew what to look for.

And he got it, still hot, a relic, a pearl. A tooth.

In that time, if only for that hour, he believed in God.

GOOD GOOD, LET'S EAT

"What about Emily?" Emmett asked. "Did she get her candy?"

Rex Henry sat across a table from him at Dear Liza's Café, the breakfast menu between them. The napkins were pink and embroidered along the selvage in green thread: "All I Need is a Little Bitta Coffee & A Whole Lotta Jesus." "Of course she did," he said.

The waitress came, and Rex Henry ordered grits for himself and biscuits and chili for the young man.

Emmett played with his napkin. He was dubious. "How'd you get it to her? You just came up to the door and said, *Special delivery?*"

"Not in so many words, no." Rex Henry stirred honey into his coffee and watched as Emmett did the same. "That is, I didn't say a word."

Emmett manufactured, as best he could, the things that followed the burning. His imagination was keen and ever sharpening, and so putting himself there at Rex Henry's side was no trouble. And what more, what he must have felt. When had Emmett ever been able to do that? His heart swelled, for Rex Henry, for the blessed Renata. He bowed his head.

There was Rex Henry, emerging from the cedar thicket, brushing splinters from his clothes and smelling of smoke. There was Rex Henry making the slow drive to the Kitchen house, the little white brick one five miles north of the El Velo border. The sky inky. There was Rex Henry going up the walk to the little white brick house, solemn and steady, the way the armed forces did when they came to tell a mother, a wife that her soldier was gone. *Miss Kitchen, the Secretary of the Army has asked me to express his deep regret…* There was Emily's face at the door, opened a crack, then flung aside when she at last understood. Maybe there were TV sounds from inside.

The waitress put down a plate of biscuits and chili. She wanted to know if the young man was all right.

Emmett heard Rex Henry from a long way off. "He's fine. He likes to say a long grace is all."

The waitress chuckled. "Well, that is sweet. He might give my boys some lessons in that area. *Good food, good meat, good God, let's eat.* That's their blessing."

In Emmett's mind's eye, Emily Kitchen was taking the pieces of De La Rosa from one old and freckled hand. He imagined that she might drop to her knees and weep, but that seemed a bit too far off the mark, like something that happened in the movies.

He was correct; it had not happened that way. Emily had, for once in her life, now that the horror under her skin had come, stood and stared, saying nothing. She could not bring herself to weep, for it was as though she had seen this nightmare a thousand slumbers before.

What is the difference between a thing that is quiet and a thing that is ordinary?

When the waitress had gone, Emmett murmured, "Don't you worry she might say something to someone?"

"Emily?"

"Yes."

"She won't."

"No?"

"No. Not if she loves Renata Ansky. Why, look. Out there, look at that."

Emmett turned and looked. All along, up and down the Main Street, was a procession, likely a continuation of the one they had seen upon entering the county. Its marchers did not carry candles at this hour, but they came bearing gifts, mostly flowers. Girls carried them, young fresh-faced lasses from the high school; their heads were bowed, their lips tight, as though they were doing penance. Emmett had thought at first that the flowers they brought were overgrown bluebonnets. He'd never seen flowers so puffy anywhere. He asked Rex Henry what they were.

"Hydrangeas," the older man replied.

"Oh." Emmett blinked. "I went to school with a girl named Hydrangea Moore. I didn't know that was a flower, too." Though it had been a day, Hydrangea Moore and all of Eufaula seemed like pieces of someone else's life.

"Hm."

"What makes them blue?"

"Eh? What, the people?"

"No. The hydrangeas."

Rex Henry swallowed a spoonful of grits and

thought. He had the look of someone browsing library stacks; Emmett wondered if he were one of those people who read a thing and never forgot it. "Well," Rex Henry said finally, "I believe it depends on the acidity in the soil. Depending on how much you've got, the flowers can bloom blue or purple or pink. Those they've got out there must've cost a pretty penny. Hydrangeas don't grow so well in dry climates."

"Oh."

Outside, a hymn rose up from the marchers. The girls from the high school led the chorus, their voices high and soft as rays from a prism. It was slow and mournful, anyway. But Emmett realized, when he strained his ear, that it was no hymn at all.

> "…Sounds of the rude world heard in the day,
>
> Lull'd by the moonlight have all pass'd away!
>
> Beautiful dreamer, awake unto me!
>
> Beautiful dreamer, awake unto me…"

Had his mother sung that to him once when he was very small? Or had it been someone else's mother?

Rex Henry settled the bill and beckoned. Emmett followed him into the general store, where there were no hydrangeas, but irises with viscose petals. "I had one bunch of those craft hydrangeas," Vera said at the register, "but one of the little girls from the high school got it. For the service."

She pointed.

The line wound through the center of town and on into El Velo, into its own Main Street, long past where Renata Ansky had last been seen. Emmett and Rex Henry took up the rear, bearing cloth irises and joining in when the marchers began "He Leadeth Me." For seven miles, as the cedar bramble around the highway thickened and then thinned, as the signs told them that they were leaving Andermatt and entering El Velo, as people from the little roadside shacks that sold fireworks and cherry bombs came to the edge of the road to look on, none of the marchers spoke. They sang. They traded hymns and children's songs, things everyone knew, "He Leadeth Me," "Sweet By and By," "Crown Him with Many Crowns" and, maybe to lighten the mood, "Merrily We Skip Along." Emmett sang what he knew, hummed what he didn't. He thought he'd caught an odor of kindling in the air, faint ashy smells as they went. He quieted when he saw the faces of those around him brighten, slowly at first, then full of glad and ruddy cheer. It was contagious, one smile begat another—and soon there were no more tears among the marchers. They began another happy song as they went down El Velo's Main Street, *"Keep on the sunny side, always on the sunny side…*" This time, the feeling in it was the real thing, real joy.

As though, Emmett thought, they were glad she was dead.

The marchers wound down a side street and narrowed into single file.

"What're we doing now?" Emmett asked.

Rex Henry craned over the heads of the ladies in front of him. "Oh. Well, the service. Up there," he pointed. Ahead was a church, Emmett could see, quite a different make than the limestone exterior of Andermatt's Sweet Home Baptist. Here was stained glass, candles, stone angels. SAINT OSANNA OF MANTUA ROMAN CATHOLIC CHURCH. RENATA ANSKY MEMORIAL MASS SATURDAY, MAY 4th, 10 AM. Inside it was standing room only. They took their places behind the last row of pews, bathed in the rosary window's final reaches, green and gold and blue. Emmett lifted his nose; love was in the air, or myrrh from the swinging censers. The mass, while not well under way, gave the impression of having already begun. As mourners continued to pour in, an exchange had been wafting back and forth between the robed men at the altar and the congregation.

From the altar: "Have mercy on us, Lord."

From the pews: "For we have sinned against you."

From the altar: "Show us, O Lord, your mercy."

From the pews: "And grant us your salvation."

Everyone in the congregation participated in this back and forth, in such perfect unison they might have all created one voice. Emmett followed Rex Henry's lead, mimicking the cadence of the words, if not the words themselves. In that time he let his eyes wander. There were so many things to look at. When the robed men at the altar talked at length, Emmett would lean in to ask Rex Henry which angel that was in the rosary window, why so many candles burned, why those people were going to the front and what was the robed man putting in their mouths.

Emmett squinted. "Is it a cracker?"

"You want to go and get some? I was just going to, myself."

"Okay."

"Are you in a state of grace?"

Emmett did not know, but he was curious. So he told Rex Henry, "Yes."

Rex Henry looked at him. "Are you sure?"

"Yes, I'm sure." He wanted that cracker, Em-

mett realized, more than any feast. He had the idea
that it would fill him up, magically, like his Aunt
Jewel, who took one mouthful of food and chewed
it thirty times. "If you eat slow enough," she would
say to his mother, "one bite of something can make
you last all day long." His mother had shed weight
that way and had called Aunt Jewel a genius. Maybe this would be like that. "Yes. I'm sure."

"All right." Rex Henry moved into the aisle.
"Keep behind me. Watch what I do."

"I thought you said you weren't devout?"

"One keeps in practice, though."

Emmett could never rightly say that he had
gone to church before. His Aunt Jewel went to
Christmas services, and his Aunt Jennie liked
to watch that program, *Life is Worth Living.* His
mother had taken him once, years ago, to Eufaula's First United Methodist. He'd been whisked
immediately from the service to the Sunday
schoolroom. The teacher was going to show the
children how to make a mosaic of the Fruits of the
Spirit, using colored paper and glue and glitter.
Emmett sat and sat and sat. The commotion, while
he couldn't specify any one child or any one voice,
was great. And so he did what he was wont to do
when the world became too much. "Miss Rachel,"
a girl had cried, "Emmett Anhalt's bleeding." And
wouldn't you know, he'd bitten his finger clear

through. That was the day his Aunt Jewel said that Emmett brought bad luck into their house. "You'll never live it down if he brings bad luck into God's house," she'd added to his mother.

How old had he been then? Seven, maybe eight. The scars on his forefinger had nearly gone; only in certain, bright sunlight could you see them. Was it too late to be redeemed, at fifteen? He did not think so.

When had he ever been a part of anything?

He shuffled behind Rex Henry, one step at a time. He absorbed the ritual: You bowed or curt-sied, just before your turn. The robed man placed the cracker, the thing, into your mouth. No one seemed to chew it, whatever it was. The recipients held it there, their throats occasionally working to moisten things, swallowed, at peace. And then they would look at one another, recognition beaming from person to person, though they might never have spoken outside of services. It was not the sort of recognition one would have for a relative or a friend, it was almost too intimate for that, too inti-mate to put into words or gestures. *We are cut from the same stuff, after all. We will have as long as we are given, no more, no less.* And wasn't that precious?

Rex Henry, in front of Emmett, stepped for-ward and met the robed man eye to eye. Beyond Rex Henry, beyond the robed man was the altar.

On it were framed photographs of a girl, hair dark and unruly, an angular face, thick brows, even as far back as her toddler pictures. Emmett didn't know what was pretty, but he wouldn't have used that word for her. But she was lovely. Yes, that's what Emmett would have said. A lovely girl. He very nearly turned to the couple in the first pew, the little couple with dark and unruly hair, the man in big bifocals, the woman in a drooping chapel veil, huddled together like birds. Emmett would have told them, "She was a lovely girl, Mr. and Mrs. Ansky. A really lovely girl. She was in a state of grace, no doubt about that."

The robed man was speaking to Rex Henry, and it was time for Emmett to pay attention.

"*Corpus Christi*," the robed man murmured.

"Ah-men," Rex Henry said, and unhinged his jaw. It made a dull crack as it closed over the little round thing the robed man had given him. He gave a great gulp, like a bullfrog, and his mouth was empty. He turned to Emmett. "I'll be outside. Just do what I did."

Emmett would ask Rex Henry what it all meant later on, and Rex Henry explained transubstantiation to him the way some parents might explain the birds and the bees to their young. It was all part of life, it all made sense. He read to Emmett a passage from the Book of Matthew, their legs overlapping in the big bed, *"Jesus took bread and blessed it, and brake it, and gave it to the disciples, and said, Take, eat; this is my body."* It was simple, and sad, and beautiful. Emmett conjured up an image of Renata Ansky, breaking a piece of De La Rosa with Emily Kitchen, with Emmett, with everyone she met, saying, "This is my body." And she would be with them always.

Emmett, at last, was glad Renata Ansky was dead, too.

He opened his mouth and swallowed her down.

"Ay-men," he croaked.

Outside, Emmett scanned the church's small vicinity until he caught sight of Rex Henry across the street. He was sitting on a bench in the little park where a trio of huge, plastic rabbits left over from Easter stood in the band shell. At his side was a girl. Her auburn hair fell down her back in hanks, as though she had neglected to comb it. She was on the short side, Emmett thought, until he saw that this was an illusion; one foot was planted on the ground, while the other scraped the grass with the toe of its Ked sneaker, one leg just longer than the other. Rex Henry reached into his pocket for another De La Rosa. The girl took it and, as Emmett thought she would, broke it. It came out in two solid pieces, not a bit of it crumbling, one for Rex Henry and one for her.

He wondered if she knew what she was doing and what it would mean.

He wondered if she was as glad as they that Renata Ansky was dead.

TERCE

Emmett looked at the books on the shelves. There were a lot of them, and the titles stuck with him because they did not seem to be organized by any order. *The Rule of Saint Benedict. Justine, or Good Conduct Well Chastised. Emily Post's Etiquette. On the Jews and Their Lies. A Little Princess.* There had never been so many books at his mother's, save for Aunt Jewel's romances. He went through four books a week here. When he was not reading, he followed Rex Henry as the older man did his chores, raking the leaves, cutting the poverty weeds from where the edge of the yard met the property line of the farmer's apple orchard next door. Rex Henry did not eat meat, but fixed Emmett venison from the freezer while he partook of black-eyed peas and rice.

It had been a month or so and Emmett did not yet know how to be in Rex Henry's house.

He felt it would be wrong to wander, for Rex Henry would worry for him. When he first arrived, Rex Henry had set up a cot for him in the room with the most books, where the walls had all around been converted into shelf space. It had been a spare bedroom when the house was built, Rex Henry told him, and now it would serve its purpose.

Emmett had always wanted to sleep alone, and now he could not do it.

He had a dream. The dream was in this very room—and it was as though he were still awake. There was a baby boy on his pillow, somewhere between the blob phase and personhood. Emmett sat bedside and listened as the baby lisped and spat. After a moment, he realized that it was hissing, *Stink, stink*. Emmett was under the impression that he'd been teaching the baby to say this. *Stink, stink, stink…*

He awoke, the sheets and pillow soaked through, and he gave the room a thorough search to make sure he was truly alone. For an hour, he sat in the middle of his cot and watched his pillow. When he could take no more of it, he got up.

Knock-knock.

"Well!" Rex Henry opened his bedroom door to a naked and shivering Emmett. The boy sat cross-legged on the floor and looked up at him like something found in a gutter. "What brings you to this neck of the woods?"

"May I stay with you?"

"What's that?"

"May I stay with you?" Emmett tried to re-member how it had been with Aunt Jennie and did what he could to make himself appealing. He let his eyes go droopy, bit the corner of his lip. "You can do whatever. Just let me stay with you."

Rex Henry, while not repulsed, did not seem eager to jump for the boy all at once. He took a step back, to look Emmett over top to toe. "But what's wrong with your own room? Is it too hot in there?"

"No."

"Too cold?"

"No."

"Something went bump in the night? That it?"

"Sort of." Emmett let himself fall forward on his knees so that his forehead pressed against the older man's belly. "Bad dream." He dug his fingers into Rex Henry's flannel pajamas. "I can't go back in there."

"Well."

Rex Henry stood for a full minute. He was completely solid. But Emmett could not, would not unhook his fingers for anything. A vehicle tootled down the dark road, headlights casting spectrally along the ceiling. In that minute, Emmett felt the world in its easiest form come back to him, and he let his hands loosen. He turned to watch the car move down the road through the picture window in the living room. He thought that he might be able to go back to his own room, but Rex Henry swooped down and lifted him up, body and soul, and brought him to the master bed. Emmett was nearly as tall as he but became like an infant in the older man's arms.

"You can pick me up," Emmett whispered. It was observation, admiration, consent.

"I can." Rex Henry laid him in the big bed, leaned over him.

Afterward, Rex Henry read to him from the stack of books on the bedside table. From one o'clock to half-past, he went through a dusty copy of *The Lives of the Saints*. Emmett seemed to enjoy Saint Seraphia's plight the most: condemned to burn, did not burn, condemned to beheading, whereupon the Almighty crowned her at last. And there were many more like her, Saint Agnes, Saint Agatha, Saint Colette, beheaded, burned, bedeviled.

"And we'll have to stop there for tonight." Rex Henry shut the book. "Busy days to follow. Best get some shut-eye."

"A little bit longer."

"All right. But this is it." Rex Henry let *The Lives of the Saints* drop next to the bed and reached for another volume. He propped it against his chest. *"Be ye therefore followers of God, as dear children…"*

Emmett tried to hang onto the words, his wakefulness grasping like smoky fingers. He was sleepy and cooled. There had been more, about filth, covetousness, whoremongering and vain words. He'd heard such phrases before, from his aunts and his mother, from Aunt Jennie's TV programs, and they passed by him like a smell; he knew they were there, but he could fan the air around him, and the words were gone. Now they stuck. *"See then that ye walk circumspectly, not as fools, but as wise, redeeming the time because the days are evil…"* Here was the world, on the surface no different than it had been on any other day of Emmett Anhalt's life. He could not deny, however, that something had shifted, the light, the shadows, the colors of things, like one of those optical illusion paintings. You let your eyes cross and stepped back, and you saw the little girls in the skull. It was not beautiful, no, nor outright terrible. It was a place that Emmett could navigate.

He sighed and turned into the pillow they shared. From above him, far away, he heard someone say, "And that is the end of the story. Just for tonight."

ACAPULCO

Andermatt County's drive-in movie theater sat neatly on the precarious border between the town of Andermatt and its neighbor, El Velo. The parking lot and concession stand were on the Andermatt side, the forty-by-twenty-foot screen in El Velo. The management, wanting to capitalize on this oddity, sprayed a boundary line in bright pink at the edge of the parking lot. It cast a candy-colored glow against the screen when the picture started, and it made the black-and-white films look dreamy and artsy. Kids hopped around the boundary, playing "Your Side, My Side".

It was a weekend hotspot, countywide. Andermatt had an indoor movie theater with air conditioning and Himmel Creek had a dance hall, but these were crowded, supervised, familiar territories where you knew how to get in and out. The drive-in was twenty-five acres, surrounded by live oak and cedar thickets, through which the shriek of bobcats and wild boar merged with the night's screening of *Singin' in the Rain*, the odors of blood with barbecue. Gaiety and gore. It was a real thrill, though no one could have quite said how.

It was where Delta Bohannon began to notice things. She refused dates to the drive-in, always had, for she enjoyed going to movies alone. No one thought it funny. Instead, people thought it chic. These days it seemed that she had grown more and more alone, and it was not her fault. She hadn't the time. There was simply too much to notice. There were signs in the sky, in the way words were put together in the magazines, in the colors of dresses, in the movies.

Two years ago, she'd treated herself to the Saturday night picture show, on her nineteenth birthday. She made plans with her beau for Sunday dinner, put on her green knit frock (her coziest, it was practically a sweater) and parked her Fairlane to take in Vincent Price and Eva Gabor.

What had it all been like before? It was how Delta gauged time now, Before and After her nineteenth birthday. Before, she had simply gone along. She had been a secretary with the Andermatt County Department of Water and Power. She had kept a little apartment in Elam, in the same building as Taylor, her beau. She followed recipes for peanut butter cookies and did not puzzle over the letters in the words. She took night classes at Schreiner and could make the drive to Kerrville, no problem.

These days, she lived under her parents' roof. Had Taylor not found her on the ranch road leading to the main highway, she might have kept walking. Taylor mapped that night out for her. She'd left her car in the drive-in lot. She could not recall having left her car. She was frightened, Taylor later told her. What of? Delta had asked him. Taylor, flustered, shrugged and said, "The movie. You were going on about how the people on the screen were looking at you. Not anything scary *in* the movie. Just how they were looking at you all the time. The manager saw you rush out."

Later, when she was all right, she wondered about where she might have ended up, had she been missed. Into the brush? Washed up with the rest of the human dregs in some back alley, trembling, blank, idiotic?

She surveyed this bedroom in her mother's house, a room that did and did not belong to her. When she moved out, her mother had sighed that they might as well do it all over as a guest room. But not a thing had been touched. Rather, things were unearthed from basement strata, dolls and tea sets, relics of childhood that Delta thought were buried forever. When she came back, it was as though she had never left, had never left and now never would. It all crept over her like kudzu vine, the eyelet coverlet and curtains, the collection of Oz books, the hobby horse, the dollhouse and its residents, a little family made from clothespins. They had yarn hair and calico dresses and suits. When Delta was small, she had called them the Holliday family. There was Mumum, Daddy, Baby, Sissy, and Sonny.

It made her clammy to revisit this piece of herself. Back then, she could pull away from the metamorphosis and put it right. The Holliday family were clothespins again. Things were things. Books held no hidden meanings. She could go along. Delta Bohannon was more ready for the world at seven than at twenty-one. Now things shifted, and she couldn't say how.

"What she needs is just some time," she heard her father murmur to her mother. The house was old, the walls wafer-thin. "Some time at home to recover. School, work—you can't juggle all that without cracking. No respite, what do you expect?"

Her mother whispered something. Her father asked her mother to repeat it. Her mother tried again, one word this time: "Saul."

Her father sighed. "Your brother heard voices. It was quite different."

"That was only one part of it—"

"Rose—"

"He said he thought the man on the radio was talking to him. That's how it started. That was how it all started."

Monday, Uncle Saul heard Eddie Cantor talk to him through a shampoo ad, *"Hay-lo, everybody, Hay-lo!"* Wednesday, the Lord was putting hidden code into the text of the *Ladies' Home Journal*. Friday, a rabbit told him to shoot his mother's French bulldog. Sunday, he fell on a carving knife. That was the legend of Uncle Saul.

Nothing talked to her. That was something. They only looked at her.

Her days fell into a pattern, one that she had quickly grown accustomed to and did not break. In time, she could not let it break. Things shifted and lifted. If she kept the pattern, things could be kept at bay, if still close by. She woke at nine and tried to take a bite of toast. She walked with her mother to the end of the road, to the mailboxes, and back. Because she could no longer read, her mother read to her. Taylor came at supper and coaxed her into one more bite. He brushed her blonde hair and trimmed the ends when they got ratty. Her father brought her for another walk in the evening, at first with the family mongrel, Sue-Sue, then (perhaps remembering what had happened to Grandma's French bulldog) he and Delta alone. He did most of the talking. Mother did the reading. Taylor did the coaxing.

Delta could not talk, could not read, could not eat. If she spoke, read, ate, if she deviated from the pattern, things would come closer. When she spoke, things she meant to say did not come out. It made her think of a fairy tale her mother read to her, the one in which toads and vipers fell from the lips of the wicked sister, rubies and roses from the good. Things came out, not real words. "Wheelbarrow," Delta would say on her morning walk. "I want to eat a penny loafer." She hadn't wanted to eat anything. She'd wanted to go back indoors, for sunlight hurt her eyes, not like Before, where she'd been warned against sun tanning so much. Her tongue betrayed her, with wheelbarrows and penny loafers. For a little while, she knew as well as anyone else that she must sound just plain batty.

How much longer would she have that?

When Saturday night came, she reached an impasse. Her head, she felt certain, would crack if she did not leave the house. She could not ask her parents or Taylor to accompany her, wherever she wanted to go. Things were manageable, even made sense. On these nights, it was as though things, all this, were nothing more than a puzzle to be worked. To expel things, Delta Bohannon would have only to delve further and further, not keep things at bay.

So she went to the drive-in. She had to, while she could still drive.

She parked the Fairlane. She told the man at the concession stand, "I want a skinned cat."

The man stared, the corners of his lips perking. He waited for the punchline, and when one did not come, he provided one. "We got a good brisket sandwich. At least, that's how we advertise it."

"Okay. I'll take that."

"Anything to drink, sweetheart?"

"Acapulco."

Fortunately, the man understood, more likely misheard. "Coca Cola, yes, ma'am."

It was a double feature, *Women's Prison* followed by *Teenage Devil Dolls*. Both were steamy pictures, bad girls who sighed and laughed and fainted and shrieked.

Sometimes they looked at her, in the way of someone trying to catch your eye across a room. Delta could no longer deny that it must be a signal, for no one else seemed to notice. The girls onscreen never looked at anyone else. Sometimes

they threw her a word, *happy, she, tease, see, can't.*
Delta couldn't piece the words together; it all
came at her so quickly. *She, split, no, want.* They
cast her a look, a word, and then it seemed the
girls, pink and aglow and unreachable, would wait
to see what Delta Bohannon would do. It was like
cracking a hangman's game, she realized, so giddy
her hands flapped. It was at the tip of her tongue,
the message, the hangman's word. If she solved it,
she would have her answer, to the confusion, the
scramble of the world, the underlying *something*
that everyone believed in, whether it was God and
angels or lost cosmonauts, the things that connect-
ed an individual to the teeming masses. And she
knew the answer must be on the tip of her tongue.

Delta Bohannon laughed and laughed and
laughed.

SEXT

"Why's she laughing?" Emmett asked. "Nothing's funny." It was his first night in Andermatt County, and he had never seen a mad person before, not in real life.

Over time, this place became their haunt. They caught every picture. If that night's show did not please them, they listened to the radio, or Rex Henry would read to Emmett. They would settle into their seats, sharing a box of Cracker Jack. Now and then, they would keep an eye on the Fairlane parked in front of them. "Watch her," Rex Henry had said. "Don't poke fun." They went to the drive-in every Saturday night, parked the Chevrolet in the same spot when they could. The

Fairlane and the girl who drove it never failed to appear.

"I wasn't poking fun," Emmett countered. He'd read *Jane Eyre* and remembered Mrs. Rochester, locked away in the great manor house and haunting its rooms a cackling, frazzled hag. The poor lady, her only way out being the long jump from the manor's roof. He tried to imagine Mrs. Rochester at Thornfield Hall. Instead, here was Aunt Jennie teetering from a Eufaula apartment house. Was Aunt Jennie mad? She'd jumped, but survived. Might the Anhalts have lived, if not happily, then bearably ever after, if she'd died?

"She sees things we don't." Rex Henry sipped from his Big Red. "Remember Joan of Arc."

It took Emmett a moment to remember that he meant the girl in the Fairlane. But perhaps he meant Aunt Jennie, too.

"She burned," Emmett said of St. Joan.

"She saved France." Rex Henry dug into the red and white Cracker Jack box, extracted the prize. It was a tin Dalmatian wearing a fireman's hat.

From the concession stand came many fragrances, of brisket from the smokers, pork from the grills. Many years ago, as a boy in Eufaula, he and his mother had lived across the street from a large family, the Hollidays. They had three children; Emmett never learned their names, but to himself, he called them Baby Easter, Christmas-Anne, and Valentino. One night, in dry midwinter, the house burned to the ground. First a lick of flame, then a damning blaze. The fire department blamed the fact that Mr. Holliday had not banked the ashes on the hearth before retiring. Neighbors crowded in the house's glow to warm their hands, to bask in the familiar odors of roasting meat wafting from inside. There was horror, yes, but it could not be denied that if you closed your eyes, you could very easily imagine yourself at a cookout, and you could not shake a feeling of coziness for a long time afterward.

Joan of Arc had smelled of pork. Emmett wouldn't say this out loud. It didn't sound right.

In the Fairlane, the girl stirred. "Acapulco," they heard her mutter.

Rex Henry said again, "Watch her." He picked a peanut from a cluster of Cracker Jack and dropped it into his Big Red, drank it down. Emmett did the same, watching the peanut sizzle at the bottom of the bottle. In Eufaula, people drank cold pop with peanuts plunked into the bottles, but Eufaula didn't have Big Red.

During the newsreel, Emmett got out of the Chevrolet pickup and walked around. He edged a little way into the cedar thicket. It was dark, and he stepped on the remains of a cat. It was gutted, its head all but torn away.

They began watching Delta Bohannon in May, and watched her still into summer's dog days. Her eyes had taken a foggy look, her speech flat. Some days she seemed to snap out of it, as from a dream upon waking, and she would take a little time to reorient herself with the world around her. Her beau, a nice-looking boy whose name Rex Henry and Emmett learned was Taylor, would take her out on the town. People knew of her, referred to "Delta's spells" over any other word.

Rex Henry, very tactfully, asked about her one night as he and Emmett were having supper at Dear Liza's.

"Well," the waitress sighed, "she's been having some spells. Her uncle had them, too." She put down scrambled eggs and tomatoes for Rex Henry, chicken pot pie for Emmett.

"How's that?"

The waitress handed Rex Henry an extra napkin and murmured, "I shouldn't say too much. She's a real doll, ever so sweet." Her voice dropped, just above a whisper. "And she's here as we speak."

"Is she?"

"That blonde, in the green dress? She's sitting there by the window with that young man?" The waitress dipped her head vaguely over her shoulder.

At the smallest table, the one with the tall, café-style legs with tall chairs to match, sat that blonde, picking at a kolache. The pastry was frazzled to crumbs around the plate. She swallowed only when the young man across from her coaxed, "Just one more bite. It's cream cheese, your favorite." After a minute, the young man got up and dropped his pocket change into the jukebox. Bing Crosby singing "Stranger in Paradise." The young man scooted his chair to Delta's side of the table and eased her against him; her head drooped over his shoulder, her face curtained by her hair. They heard her croak "Taylor" as though she had only now recognized him and was still unsure. "Are you the real one? You're not going away?"

The young man nodded, quickly, his face puffy. He pressed his face against the crown of her head.

Emmett put his fork down. Rex Henry handed him a napkin and said, "Try and blow your nose. I know. It's something. But blow your nose."

Bing Crosby sang, *"I saw her face, and I ascended…out of the common place…"*

Here was a true devotee, this young man. Emmett puzzled at the stuff fidelity was made of. There was the old saying, "Absence makes the heart grow fonder." And its opposite, "Out of sight, out of mind." The former stung, so suddenly and with such venom that he half-expected it to be felt by those around him. But the pain was all his—at least, it felt that way. Here was Emmett, who had, until now, never been cherished. Devotion of one soul for another was the stuff of books. People put up with one another, lumps of bolus who shared the same space. And here was a miracle: a boy worshipping at Delta Bohannon's scent, her dear hair. When she was gone, he would be left. No one knew her the way he did.

What makes the difference between a thing that is quiet and a thing that is ordinary?

How would Rex Henry answer if Emmett were to tell him, *I love you?* Most people would repeat you, like a trained parrot. *I love you I love you I love you.* But Rex Henry wasn't like that.

It made Emmett want to rejoice. It made him angry. That was the thing about Rex Henry, he knew: he could go along with Emmett or without. About this, Emmett did not fool himself. Emmett knew what would become of him if Rex Henry were to up and vanish, no question. Rex Henry Burr would not die. Rex Henry Burr would return to the ether, just as he had come. Emmett Anhalt would die. Emmett Anhalt would go into ground, for what else would there be for him? He lived day to day, and Rex Henry was the sun—and there he bloomed.

The taste of self-pity was sweet, and he luxuriated.

Rex Henry's hand on his shoulder. He had paid the bill and was leading him outside. He was pressing a red bandana against Emmett's knuckle. "I know. It's something. But you've gotta know when to dial it back."

When he pulled his hand back, Emmett saw that it was not covered with a bandana but a hankie, blood-soaked. He'd bitten his finger through.

SUMMERLAND

In August, Rex Henry told him to think about Paradise. "What does that mean to you? What do you think about when you hear that?"

They were in Rex Henry's bed, and because Emmett could think of nowhere else he'd rather be, he said, "Right here."

Rex Henry chuckled. "Well, I'm very flattered. But I was thinking of what it meant to you alone. Something that's all yours."

Emmett thought, and he found that he did not have to grasp for it.

It was Memorial Day weekend, not long after he had seen Delta Bohannon for the first time. Rex

Henry had guessed, rightly, that Emmett would not take to the cheering masses that congregated roadside for the Andermatt County parade. "It is bacchanalia," Rex Henry had said of it: the candies pelted at the spectators, the greedy children clamoring for them, the Miss Bluebonnet pageant winners in all their glitter and vice. "It's not something you need to see." Instead, they went for a long drive. They did not go far. They took the pickup around and around until Emmett could feel the pattern of their journey: a figure-eight. In Himmel Creek was open land, rolling grass like the ocean's bottom, the only life beyond the highway being the oil rigs in the distance and the Missouri-Kansas-Texas Railroad hauling freight.

But, wouldn't you know, like an oasis out where not even a firework salesman would set up shop, there was a little funfair. It was more of a playground, really; there were swings and a see-saw. But it had a carnival element also; it had a merry-go-round and a Little Engine That Could on a track that wound all around the park. The place sold hot dogs and apples dipped in cajeta and chopped peanuts. A loudspeaker played music from *The Magic Flute*. Rex Henry and Emmett had the place to themselves, and they did not question why the park would be open on a holiday. On the merry-go-round, Emmett mounted a hare with gilded ears, Rex Henry an elk painted green and pink. Around them the world became a green and gold hodgepodge, and the air tasted of cajeta. Rex Henry whistled part of "Der Holle Rache." It was, simply, a good day. Probably Emmett's best.

And he told Rex Henry so. He added, "We've never gone back. Couldn't we go back?"

"Well, of course." Rex Henry nodded, his hand in Emmett's hair. "If it's still there."

"Why wouldn't it be?" It occurred to Emmett that this was the one part of the long drive that he hadn't tracked. It seemed to be in a fugue place. He tried to recall any surrounding landmarks: the oil rigs, the MKT Railroad running through the empty grass along the highway. They had stopped for ice cream beyond the Himmel Creek limits, a shabby seasonal place that made the best butter pecan either of them had ever had. But even that seemed unlikely, like something Emmett had dreamed.

"Summer has ended," Rex Henry said, solemn. "Just about. Places like that are usually open from late spring to just before Labor Day."

...the summer is ended, and we are not saved.

Was Paradise not something to which Emmett could return? Or was it like that day, one taste and that was it?

"Well," Rex Henry said, "there will be more.

Always there will be. You just have to be patient. Be good and be patient. It'll be back next year and you'll go. Provided you don't act up."

Emmett resented that. He was as a loyal watchdog. He did not speak unless he was spoken to. He followed without argument. He submitted. He held no one above Rex Henry. "I don't act up," he mumbled.

"What'd I hear?"

Emmett knew better than to repeat himself. He did meet Rex Henry's eye when he said, "When do we get up?"

Rex Henry gave him a long look. His face never changed, never creased or reddened. He simply held you with his eyes until you had to look at him and know his permanence. "Quarter to six," he said finally. "We leave at half past seven. Does that suit you?"

"Yes." Emmett rolled into his side of the pillow.

Then from the pillow's other side, "Keep thinking about Paradise."

"What does it have to do with me?"

DELTA PARADISE

Delta Bohannon thought about Paradise, more and more.

She had come to the conclusion that the world as she knew it was separated from its neighboring dimensions by veil-thin barriers. Now and then, clues to the other side would crop up. At first, it all came to her through the meanings in single words, puzzles to be solved in the things people said to one another, in the phrasings of magazine ads. She unearthed her scrapbook from high school, tore out the dance cards and recipes, the snapshots and newspaper honor roll columns, and filled it with clippings. She pored over everything she could, issues of *Mademoiselle* and *The*

Reader's Digest, The Ladies' Home Journal, Sears & Roebuck catalogs, pieces of the *Statesman.* Words and individual letters highlighted in red and inked with stars and connecting lines. There was an intricacy to it that made her think of those optical illusion pictures; you strain your eyes and pull the picture back until the image pops out at you. She did something like that now, and individual letters in different paragraphs came together to form words. Once, she caught a sentence; she'd had the foresight, even in her confusion, to write it in the margin of an *Andermatt Courant* article. Big, block letters: "THEY LOVE ME."

It made sense when she'd put the scrapbook together.

Her lap was full of scraps of paper.

Today was one of her Good Days. She spread the scrapbook across her lap and gazed at its contents in horror. Then the horror would fade into something cold and inert. On her Good Days, things fell back into place, to be sure, but left her empty. Bad Days, though ugly, gave her purpose. She was not Delta Bohannon, that Poor Dear. She was Delta, the Oracle; Delta of Many Colors; Delta the Just; the Blessed Delta. Delta Bohannon had gone as far as she would go in this world.

Since her illness, her days had been more or less the same, and so she ought to be able to say the same for Sundays. Sundays were at-home days. The family all had dinner together on Sundays. Dad grilled quail, Mother fixed twice-baked potatoes, Taylor brought a dessert. Every day but Sunday, Delta took her meals in her bedroom. On that day, of all days, she would take her old place at the table, where Dad, Mother, and Taylor would watch her eat.

She could stand others looking at her; other people did not belong to her the way her parents, her beau, did. They looked at her and watched her eat. They ferried words to each other, which were ferried to Delta, and they would look to see if she could piece together what they truly meant to say.

A Good Day going Bad, like watching a light recede down a dark hallway.

Dad passed the succotash and said, "Her."

Mother took a bite of potato and said, "Those two do."

Taylor mopped his lips and said, "Love."

They looked at her, eyes wide. In awe? What in her had they seen? Resplendency made a slow course through the back of her head, welling in her groin. The room seemed larger, the light fuller and not as sharp. She was no longer afraid, and the idea that she had cause to ever be seemed silly.

They ought to look at her.

They knew what she was made of.

The pleasure of it made her gasp, and it rippled with laughter.

She was Paradise.

From the head of the table, Mr. Bohannon murmured, "Rose, take her—" And he got up and ushered Taylor into the den to watch TV.

Mother moved to her daughter's side of the table, to pull Delta's hand out from her corduroys, to pick up the plate she had overturned, to wipe the dampness from her daughter's bleary eyes.

THE CENTER

Rex Henry and Emmett sat for eight o'clock Mass and received Communion. They walked the little turf maze in the church's courtyard, and Rex Henry explained to Emmett that this was really a path to the Holy Land: "Pilgrims walked this if they couldn't make the trip to Jerusalem." They went to Dear Liza's for breakfast, where Emmett had a little thin toast and orange juice. Rex Henry had tea, nothing else. They were fasting.

"You're young yet to do a real fast," Rex Henry said as they went back to the pickup. "And it won't do to have you falling down all over the place." He instructed Emmett to drink plenty of water throughout the day. He'd placed four full canteens in the back of the cab. Then he dug into the glove compartment. "Trail mix. It won't fail the astronauts, and it won't fail you."

"I'll keep pure," Emmett said around a bite.

Rex Henry nodded. "And you won't be falling down."

"That wouldn't do."

"No, it wouldn't."

They went for another drive, much shorter this time. The day was frothy and green, made all the more so because the county was due for a storm. The creek beds around the edges of town were nearly sapped of their flow, and stood now to divide the land like gorges. For a week, since the schools opened again, time passed heavily, overcast, moist, tight. Not a drop of rain in two months and constant teasing of heat lightning. *The center cannot hold*, as the mystics said. Indeed, the county was due.

They passed the post office, where Ivo Ansky still received flowers as tribute to the Blessed Renata, his daughter. They passed a field in which many white goats rutted in the dry grass. A llama knelt in their midst, its neck drooping as though the animal were about to wilt. A firework hut opening its pink shutters, ready for business now that the burn ban was lifted, what with the coming rain.

Rex Henry whistled along with the radio and taught Emmett the tune, "Der Hölle Rache." Emmett had never whistled before and, for a first timer, he wasn't half bad. It kept his mind off the bag of trail mix and what was to come in the day. But he allowed himself a handful of oats and peanuts, another sip of water.

He whistled until Rex Henry parked. He did not recognize where they were because he had never been to the drive-in during the day; he had no reason to believe that it would be there. The screen was blank, the lot empty but for a dallying odor of scorched fat.

Tonight's movie starred Shirley Temple, *A Little Princess*.

Emmett was excited, frightened, too. He felt he ought to say something. He blurted, "I read the book of that."

"I know. It's a good one."

"Will we see it?"

"If there's time. We've got things to do."

The slam of the pickup's doors clapped around them in that thicket of cedar. Emmett caught the beginning of a sound, something rough like a grunt, then the sound of tiny hooves galloping away into the brush. A boar, Rex Henry noted, as they drew themselves into the trees and bramble.

A few steps in and the drive-in lot had vanished, as had the sounds of the adjacent highways. The smell of meat was still thick, but it was not smoky. All was still and all was stirring.

Their feet met tarmac, an empty highway. At first, all Emmett could see was a wash of grass, bisected by a railroad. Then, rising like a bony offering out of the green, the oil rig. His head swept right to left, for he knew where he was, and there, there a little way down the road, a flash of color. There was the funfair, the merry-go-round rotating slowly. Mozart was swapped for conjunto music.

Rex Henry said, "I know what you're thinking." He likely knew the number of hairs on Emmett's head. "Not until after. Things to do, remember, and we've got to prepare for them. If we're going to do this, we've got to keep our heads clear."

"What'll we do?"

"We'll just walk."

"*Walk.*"

"Yes, walk. That's all."

And they moved beyond the funfair with its burnt sugar smell and its accordion notes. Emmett looked with longing at the merry-go-round's hare with gilded ears, but he kept going. Now and then a car would wind down the road, slow, just below the speed limit. The driver rippled a wave at Rex Henry, called, "Have a blest day." Another car came and did the same, disappeared into the hazy horizon. Not one stopped to offer a ride, as many had for Emmett in his wandering Eufaula days. To his knowledge, they had no destination. What might they have said if they had been picked up? *Take me to the end of the earth?*

Emmett sweated, but could not say that he was tired. He occupied his mind with little tricks, riddles he remembered. He told one to Rex Henry: *You are driving a bus. At the first stop, four people get off. At the second stop, one person gets off. At the third stop, eight people get off. At the last stop, everyone gets off. The question: How old is the bus driver?* It was part brain-teaser, part ploy; he wondered if Rex Henry would tell him how old he was. Instead, Rex Henry told him, "I'd always heard that one as, *What color are the bus driver's eyes?* It's a good little mystery, but we really ought to have it quiet just now."

And so Emmett kept his amusements to himself, counting trees, picking wildflowers. In time, his mind quieted and smoothed and he abandoned the riddles, allowing himself to become a perfect mechanism. His limbs went up and down, no agency other than the blessing of continuous movement, on and on. His mind dimmed and he did not speak. Emmett Anhalt could go forth this way, into the Gulf of Mexico and marching along the ocean's surface until he reached the Strait of Gibraltar. And he would keep going, until Rex Henry told him to stop. A mile down the road, further into the green, and Emmett thought that this was the point at which the world dropped off, when Rex Henry put out a finger. "Up there."

There were more like them, just ahead. Mostly girls, a few men, many women.

There were four girls ahead, about Emmett's age, trailing in the wake of a dowdy little thing with red hair and a limp. Emmett blinked and a name surfaced: It was Emily Kitchen, whom the Blessed Renata had loved. The quartet who followed her looked on from the corners of their eyes, murmuring into the thick air. They looked ready to drop at any moment, flushed, drenched in their own liquids. They were not as plump as they had been the last time they saw Renata Ansky, at Phillip D. Andermatt High School. Unbeknownst to Emmett, they were also on a fast. (For the last month, Maxine and Glenda and Willie and Kay had decided to give up meat. Then dairy. Then sweets. Then fruit. At last, they had reduced themselves to twiggy penitents who subsided on water and canned tuna fish. They would never say a foul word about anyone again.)

The others ahead kept their heads down. They watched their feet. They carried arrangements of cheap craft hydrangeas. They did not sing this time, or talk amongst themselves. It was very like the walk along the turf maze at the church, where you retreated into your core and there you stayed until it was time to stop.

They came to a plywood sign, painted purple and white, set up beneath the speed limit marker. It read, in blocky letters with curlicues: RENATA'S WALK. Then, in smaller letters, THY WORD IS A LAMP UNTO MY FEET, AND A LIGHT UNTO MY PATH. PSALMS 119:105. There, the devotees laid their bouquets and curtsied or bowed. The four girls watched as Emily Kitchen knelt to make her offering, a single De La Rosa candy, slightly crushed inside the wrapping. They curtsied.

And they all went on and on, as the sky darkened and sank and finally gave way. Heavily washed and heavily clean, they could only keep going.

Emmett wondered what Delta Bohannon's memorial would be like.

TRANSUBSTANTIATION

Renata Ansky did not have a burial because there was no body. Ivo and Laura Ansky could not quite bring themselves to do anything symbolic, a headstone at the Andermatt Garden of Memories. The shrines that appeared countywide were good enough, they would say. Privately, they preferred the idea of an Assumption, body and soul, into Paradise.

Delta Bohannon had one piece left behind, something she'd neglected to take with her to the other side. While the rest of her vanished, all who knew her had to be content with her smallest toe.

Dennis and Rose Bohannon had a mongrel, Sue-Sue, part Basset hound, part Catahoula, part pointer, and a drop of German shepherd. She made for an odd-looking animal: stumpy legs, a long figure, thick and bridle-colored like a sausage, round eyes set widely apart, flat paws. "God was reading the funnies when he made this one," Dennis Bohannon said and patted her. Sue-Sue liked to roam and, because her masters trusted her, they let her. She slept outdoors, and so escapes were that much easier. She could disappear for days at a time, for her sojourns took her far. More than once, a rancher would call to say that she'd been vexing his goats: "If she didn't keep the armadillos away, I'd shoot. When're you coming to get this damn dog?"

Like the devotees who made Renata's Walk, Sue-Sue was a marathoner, no destination but a renewed peace of heart.

The prime, up-and-go hour was Sunday, dinnertime. The family sat and ate and was often too full to leave the house for the rest of the night. Now that the rain had stopped, Dennis Bohannon got up from where he was watching television with Delta's beau and let Sue-Sue out into the yard.

On this day, she had wedged herself into the hollow she'd dug beneath the Bohannon's fence. No one had filled it yet. She padded to the end of the drive to the mailboxes and sat to huff at the air. For a while, she watched cars pass. A fly teased her snout, her eyes, her ears, and when it alighted on her lips, she snapped at it and ate it. Then she moseyed down the road.

As a pup her tail had been docked, and so when she felt any particular excitement, joy, hunger, anticipation, her rump gave a funny, phantom twitch. She paused at a low concrete bridge that stood over a creek, one that had been nearly dry until this morning. Now it ran lively, unclogging a summer-long buildup of bramble. She sat and looked at the flow and took in the air again. She cast her legs to one side to allow her rump to twitch and jitter.

It was still summer and the sun had not yet set. The coming Fairlane did not use its headlights, though the sky had gone in this short time from pink to red. It lurched across the little bridge, almost too wide to be contained. The driver did not see Sue-Sue, for the mongrel could be quick on her feet; she dove into the muddy creek before the Fairlane could cross. She emerged, swampy and bramble-spiked, to give a rough howl at the shore. And she took off at a full gallop, for the driver was Delta and there had been a time, she foggily recalled, when Delta took her hither and yon in that car. The trailing air was full of Delta, her favorite, of her meat smell. It had been ages since Sue-Sue had been let to see her. She wanted to taste her, her favorite.

The Fairlane was old and was not inclined to go above thirty-five miles per hour. It grunted over

113

the El Velo town line and through a neighbor-hood where all the houses were small but had wide porches.

April Nimitz, who lived in the blue house, sat on the steps, airing herself in between weeding her flowerbeds. She ran her handkerchief through the hose and plopped it on the crown of her head. A moment passed in which she closed her eyes and centered herself. The world around her seemed to still this way: the radio from inside, her little girl and her husband singing along with that shampoo jingle *("Hay-lo, everybody, Hay-lo!")*, a cicada, then two, then ten. *A something in a summer's day / As her slow flambeaux burn away.* Who said it? She wasn't normally a fan of poetry, but she remembered liking this one. Who said it?

When she woke, it was to a world through which a Fairlane cranked and a mongrel yapped and yowled in its wake.

"Hey, Juan," she called, "Juan, babe. Better call Dennis and Rose. That dog's out."

"I'll get to it when I get to it," came the reply.

April sighed and draped the hankie over her face. "You better." *Dickinson,* she thought. *That sainted little shut-in.*

The mongrel, Sue-Sue, panted and panted. She thought, *I love you I love you I love you—*

GETHSEMANE

In the cedar thicket, washed and pure, Rex Henry and Emmett knelt over the thorns and meditated. Emmett's hands trembled, and the older man handed him the bag of trail mix. "Get some of that down," he said. "But keep your mind clear."

And Emmett did. He thought of all the saviors he'd had and never knew, how he might never have known them if they had gone on, undisturbed, never caught. Saint Paul could have lived forever, and were he not beheaded in Rome, would his missions, up and down the world itself, have held the same succor for all who heard him? *The Pearl of Great Price.* It was something that Rex Henry was always saying, and it was now that Emmett felt he was beginning to understand it.

The sainted ones made the world glow. It didn't matter who they were caught by, Emmett reasoned. Anything that happened to them, no matter how awful (and somehow, the more awful their fate, the better), was part of a plan. Anything that deviated from the plan set the way of things in a great imbalance.

But Emmett could not make his hands stop shaking.

Rex Henry grasped for them, held them still. His palms were small, but the fingers long; they wrapped around Emmett's paws like petals on a rose.

Rex Henry said, "Remember. The executioner is always forgiven."

They had brought Buck knives and kindling. If anyone came upon them in the woods, they told them they were hunting white tail.

EL AUTO

The Fairlane sat in the drive-in long before the crowds came.

The families pulled in early to claim good spots. Their children's faces were sticky with cajeta and they waved empty sticks, the candied apples gnawed away. While their parents stood in line at the concession, the young ones made a beeline for the front, where the pink line stood between Andermatt and El Velo. Above them, a blank screen.

The children hopped from one foot to the other. They waved their bare sticks and chanted, "Your side, my side. Your side, my side." They spoke in abrupt little phrases, some English, some Spanish. They had figured out a new game, in which the white kids pointed to something and the Mexican kids gave it a new name.

"Whassat?"

"*El arbol.*"

"Whassat?"

"*El auto.*"

And, giggling at the outhouse at the entrance, "Whassat?"

And, giggling almost too much to say it, "*La casa de mierda.*"

They all had a grand time with that one, screeching "*La mierda! La mierda!*" until someone's mother cast a forbidding look from the concession line. It was enough to quiet them, and they resumed the game, sobered.

"Whassat?" A penny loafer, abandoned in the dead center of the lot.

"*El zapato.*" The speaker, a little girl in a red sweater, the hood pulled over her dark hair, inched closer to inspect it. She turned back to the group. "It looks brand new."

"So?"

"So, there might be a penny in it." She poked it with her candied apple stick, lifted it so that the loafer dangled from the end.

One of the white kids, a towheaded boy who whistled through the gaps of missing teeth, grew flustered. "Marilu! Don't touch it!" He hopped from foot to foot. "Put it down!"

The girl called Marilu twirled the shoe on the end of her stick. "Why?"

"Well, this one time, my brother picked up a shoe he left out on our porch—" the gap toothed boy snuffled, "—and a scorpion crawled out and stuck him five times in his hand. He was all swolled up."

The girl called Marilu grunted, her mouth twisting. "Your brother's a queer. I been stung everyplace; they get in our bathroom all the time. It doesn't hurt." She cast her arm back and flung the loafer across the parking lot, into the middle of the road. A passing Buick flattened it. "There was no penny, anyway."

"Can we keep playing?"

"No. It was getting stupid. You want to learn Spanish, watch Ricky Ricardo on the TV." The girl called Marilu pulled her hood down and unbuttoned her sweater. She waded through the rows of cars, back toward the front. The others followed, because she was the oldest (just eight), because she had charisma. She figured this early in life that if she said something, anything, in the right way, in the right tone, with such aplomb and steel that there was no room for dissent, she could sway numbers. Tens, thousands, tens of thousands. She was not pretty, but she was strong. People listened to her, even when they shouldn't. Now, she stepped between cars, a winding line of little heads behind her. No one said anything when she tried the handles of the doors; most were locked. She parroted a line she'd heard in too many movies: "There's gold in them thar hills."

The little gap-toothed boy tittered. "You mean, there's gold in them thar cars."

In the cars Marilu had opened, they found empty Coke bottles and cigarette boxes, no real loot. They soon came upon a bit of luck: The glove compartment of an unlocked Chrysler secreted a box of Russell Stover chocolates. This was, more or less, what the children would have bought with any pilfered coin, and so, huddling at the edge of the pink line by the screen, they wolfed down as many of the candies as they could before anyone saw. But they were greedier than they were hungry. Marilu pitched the candy box into the tall grass and led them to the Fairlane. "It's just sitting there. If anyone was going to come back, they would've come by now. The movie's about to start."

A little boy, clopping forward in cowboy boots a size too big, knelt and craned his head. He tugged at Marilu's skirt. He squeaked, *"Hay un perro."*

"What?" Marilu took her hand from the Fairlane's door's handle. *"Dónde está?"*

The white kids backed away, clustering. "What's he say? What's he say?"

The little boy in cowboy boots pointed, his finger sticky, fat, the nail bitten. *"Ahí abajo."*

The white kids, noting that the little boy's tone was one of glee and not fear, gradually spread apart and came forward on tiptoe. The gap-toothed boy whistled, "What's he say?"

Marilu got to her knees and peeked under the Fairlane. "I'll be damned," she breathed. "It's a puppy dog."

"It's not a puppy," the gap-toothed boy said, "it's too big."

The little boy with the cowboy boots cooed, *"Ven aquí, ven aqui…"*

"Come on, ol' dog, good ol' dog—"

"Pretty dog, hey, pretty dog—"

"I'll give him my hotdog. Hear that, puppy dog, I got something good for you—"

The dog beneath the Fairlane lay with her paws over her snout. Ordinarily, she could have loved the petting of so many children. But she could not open her mouth to kiss them. There was something in it she did not want to lose.

"C'mon, pretty dog—" Marilu crouched at the gap between the car and the ground, where the dog huddled. She put out her hand, tightly fisted, knuckles first, in case the dog bit. "C'mon out, ol' dog."

It was too much to bear. Like people, beasts surrender to comfort. Sue-Sue longed to be petted; she needed it. And so, wriggling on her belly, she wedged herself out from under her mistress' Fairlane and let herself be wreathed by adoring children. They fussed, they hugged, they kissed her soft ears. The little boy in cowboy boots put out his palm to see if she would shake; she did, with both paws. But she could not open her mouth to kiss them back. And she could not take the treats they offered her. She had to keep what was inside her mouth.

Finally, the children caught on.

They pawed at her snout, lifted her lips. The gap-toothed boy stepped on her hind foot and she yelped. From her mouth dropped the relic, all Sue-Sue had of her mistress, Delta Bohannon; her mistress would need her toe, if she were to return.

And as quickly as they had gathered, the children fanned away, silent, until Marilu, in a moment in which her toughness crumbled at her feet, screamed and screamed and screamed.

As Shirley Temple danced across the screen, boars rutted and bobcats yowled.

EL PERRO

Rex Henry manned the Chevrolet homeward. He looked at Emmett. "It wasn't our dog."

"I know it."

"Think how you'd feel if someone up and took your dog."

"...Awful."

"Well, all right."

"It's just that..."

"...Just that what? You're going to have to speak up."

"It's nothing."

"You're sure?"

"Yes."

"Well, all right."

Emmett had not cried in years. It had been so long he could not summon a taste of how it had felt, what or whom he had cried for, how long it had lasted before he had cried himself out. He had nothing to compare this moment to. There was sorrow for what had passed, yes, but it was tinged here and there with joy, the way stones are specked with gold. He would wait until he was completely alone, let it out then.

Rex Henry reached over to touch Emmett's face. He said, "You'll want to wash all that stuff off when we get home."

"Why?"

"Well, you want to get clean after a good day's work."

"Don't we want people to see it?"

They had come through the woods, as they were, into the drive-in's parking lot. It was as though Rex Henry had willed them invisible, for no one looked their way, save for a little girl, a little girl whose eyes were as red as her sweater. She peered out at them from beneath her hood, but even then, her gaze was foggy, like someone caught halfway between dreaming and waking. Emmett couldn't be sure if she believed what she saw.

"No. Not as yet." Rex Henry rubbed the residue between his fingers, where it rolled into grime.

Emmett squeezed his hand around his prize.

Rex Henry said, "Better put that in a safe place. Don't want to lose that. It's a special thing."

It made Emmett want to hold it, that tooth, all the more tightly. "I'll never lose it."

At home, he sat in the tub, the water hot enough to fill the room with steam. Rex Henry sat on the toilet, reading an issue of *Mademoiselle* and waiting his turn. The magazine, Emmett could see, was full of red ink, circled words, phrases underlined, whole paragraphs starred or marked with exclamation points. It hadn't made sense when they took it from Delta Bohannon, but Rex Henry pored over it as though it were the Parables.

Emmett bent over to put his face in the water, but did not submerge his ears. He heard the older man turn the pages. "I find," Rex Henry said finally, "that there is absolute consistency in this text."

Emmett sat up, water dripping into his eyes. "What?"

Rex Henry peeled the magazine open to an article on Maidenform bras. "It's puzzling at first, yes, but so simple once you've found it. Try to look beyond the stars and whatnot."

Emmett did, though he felt he had to cross his

eyes to see. He craned his neck forward and back, looking like a numb cockerel. Then, having found the perfect position, the perfect light, the ideal conditions for the madness of all that red ink to fall into place, he had it. Three words leapt out at him, all down the Maidenform article, and on into the next, this one an interview with Grandma Moses. Over and over again, a mantra:

> *They Love me they love me The y love Me they love me They love me they love me they love me they love me they love me the y love Me They Love ME they love me they love me they love me they love me*

Perhaps they had even touched upon the glamor of her mind.

Delta Bohannon had come to them an escapee from her own home. She could still drive and there were not many places left to her that could be called sacred. At the drive-in, she'd sat in the Fairlane, while Sue-Sue howled and scratched at the door, grating away the oyster-colored paint. She was meant to be here, here alone. No look, no voice had told her. She wore her green knit dress, sour-smelling now that she'd refused to take it off for anything; she'd found that whatever was meant to find her here would know her in her green dress. It was like those notes that blind dates might send to each other before the big night: *I'll be easy to spot. I'll be wearing a green knit dress.* The momentousness and the great fortunes of the world came together for her now. Big things were meant to happen. All you had to do was to be in the right place, at the right time, at the right hour, the right minute.

She'd left the car. When Sue-Sue leapt for her, Delta removed her penny loafer, the one from her right foot, and pitched it across the parking lot. Then she let the cedar woods take her.

And there they were, just as she knew they would be. A boy and a man, just standing, waiting, waiting for her. This, as it turned out, was the single thing in her illness that she had gotten right. It was as though her confusion had come to deliver her here, planted the clarity of predestination of all things. She knew in an instant, just as she knew that the sun rose and set, that this was how she would depart. They had not as yet touched her, nor spoken to her.

Then they came at her.

As she suffered, she told Emmett and Rex Henry what would become of them. She was not vengeful about it, just stating the facts. For the first time in a long time, she spoke sensibly. Through a mouthful of blood, she looked at Emmett and said, "He's gonna leave you. You'll be on your own. At the end of this, you'll be on your own." And she spat at him.

And Emmett had loved her for that. She had borne it all with the kind of grace Rex Henry had said she would. Emmett had kept in mind the story of Saint Lucy, patron of the blind and of plagues.

Rex Henry had read to him from Butler's *Lives of the Saints*: "...our Lord, by a special miracle, saved from outrage this virgin whom He had chosen for His own. The fire kindled around her did her no hurt. Then the sword was plunged into her heart, and the promise made at the tomb of St. Agatha was fulfilled." Delta Bohannon had laughed throughout her ordeal and said again and again, "They love me, they love me, they love me, they love me—" Emmett had said after her, "We love you, we love you, we love you, we love you—" When she left them, they assembled her remains, as much as they could of them, into kindling and scattered her ashes into the four winds.

It was at around that point that the dog had come.

They had petted her and gave her water from their canteens. Rex Henry let Emmett feed her some of his trail mix. She only seemed to like the peanuts. The dog then sniffed and snuffed at the smoldering remains; there were still a few pieces, relics, that they meant to keep and had put to one side. It was these things from which they had at first tried to keep her away, luring her with more peanuts, more water, a stick without cedar spines for playing fetch. Nothing took the dog away.

"We'll bring her home," Emmett had said. His face was damp and soiled; he was still basking in it.

"She's not our dog."

"She doesn't have anyplace to go back to."

"She's not our dog." Rex Henry scratched behind her ear. "I know she's a good dog. But she has a mistress."

"No, she doesn't."

"She does." Rex Henry's face was stony. "Think of Guinefort." Guinefort, the dog saint. He wasn't among those listed in Butler's *Lives*. Rex Henry had told Emmett that first night over bowls of chili at the Carnelian. Guinefort was the beloved hound of a knight, of Saint Malcolm, no less. One day, Saint Malcolm was called away from his homestead and left Guinefort to care for his infant son. The hound, upon his return, met Saint Malcolm with gore about his chops. Thinking Guinefort had eaten his only son, Saint Malcolm slew Guinefort—but came home to hear his infant son cooing just where Saint Malcolm had left him, in his cradle. And at the cradle's foot lay a gored serpent. Guinefort, having proved himself good and faithful in the eyes of his Redeemer, was returned to earth, body and soul, to protect Saint Malcolm and his brood. All who knew Guinefort came to him to be healed, to be saved.

It was a good story, Emmett thought.

But there wasn't a Saint Malcolm in Butler's *Lives*, either.

The dog had gotten hold of the toe that Emmett had particularly liked. It was the smallest toe from

135

Delta Bohannon's right foot, the nail painted shell pink. Rex Henry told Emmett to let it go. "Let her keep it. We've got plenty of our own."

"Supposing someone sees it?"

"Well. We should be so lucky. *She* should be so lucky."

Emmett couldn't say whether Rex Henry was talking about Delta Bohannon or the dog. He did not ask why the dog could not be sacrificed; he would not have been able to bear it, regardless of the good it would do.

And so, they watched the dog tear away through the bramble, yelping and grunting through the small burden in her mouth.

"She wasn't our dog," Rex Henry had said.

If she'd stayed with them, might she have saved them?

Emmett asked Rex Henry this from his place in the bathtub. The claggy air and the aroma of Halo shampoo made him bold.

Rex Henry looked from him, to the magazine drooping over his knee, to the copied portrait of Chief Quanah Parker that hung next to the medicine cabinet. "It's not likely."

"Why's that?"

"You don't need it. You never have."

"She said you would leave me." Emmett had cleaned the bloodspittle from his face, though the warmth of it lingered.

"I will, yes."

"When will that be?"

Rex Henry got to his feet, went to straighten the portrait of the chief. Quanah Parker gazed out at them, his eyes steely. He did not look the way Emmet imagined a Comanche to be; he wore a suit and a sort of bowler hat, though his hair was long and braided.

Rex Henry turned and said, "I can't say that." Then he bent to root in the linen closet for a towel. "Come on. You've been in there so long, you're liable to be a prune."

They did not go to Delta Bohannon's memorial service at the Sweet Home Baptist Church. Nor did they go for breakfast at Dear Liza's, or to the funfair. They stuck close to home for a good few months afterward. Rex Henry had an above-ground root cellar and he kept it well-stocked. From August to October, they lived on rice and preserves, canned stews, powdered milk, venison jerky, and Hershey bars. Emmett particularly liked cactus fruit jelly over crackers; it was like honey, and it left a floral tang at the back of his tongue.

The yard stretched for miles. Rex Henry owned close to one hundred acres and, up to the edge of the apple orchard, all was his from horizon to horizon.

Emmett wandered, bare, at dusk. He sat under the patches of sunflowers that grew wild, or he walked and read aloud to himself. He was on *The Rule of St Benedict* now. It was short, so he could read it again and again. Life at Rex Henry's was not unlike the way of a monastery. What kind of monk did Emmett make? A cenobite, who served under the rule of a holy man? Or an anchorite, whose only company was divine? To answer that question was to know what Rex Henry was made of, and this Emmett could not begin to guess.

It seemed to him, more and more, that Rex Henry had never been a child. He had never been a young man, like Emmett. He had never and would never be very old. He had always been. He had an answer for anything. Emmett did not want to know about the ways of the universe; he wanted to know about himself. One day, he asked Rex Henry if he knew the number of hairs on his head. Rex Henry nodded and, without a beat, said, "One hundred-and-fifty-two-thousand, six hundred-and-thirty-nine." Emmett asked if he had been an only child, right from the beginning, or if he had any brothers or sisters, who had come or gone before their time. Rex Henry told him to feel the knob at the back of his neck, where the shoulders joined. "You would have had a twin, a sister. In the womb, you were hungry and absorbed her. Now you carry what is left of her always. That is your burden." It took Emmett a moment to process this, but soon, he was back at it, more and more about his person that remained a mystery. For instance, did his mother love him? His aunts? Rex Henry, as Emmett thought he might, shook his head; no one could love him as Rex Henry did, and nothing could compare.

In the bathroom, Emmett fingered the knob at the back of his neck. He'd thought that everyone had one, as far as he could see.

He could not bring himself to ask the most important question. It rose at the back of his throat like vomit, and he always managed to choke it back down. He wanted to know, *When will I die?* He felt that this was something he could easily find out himself, the date, the hour tucked away in the chambers of his heart. Emmett knew the circumstances; he didn't have to grope for that. Delta Bohannon had told him to his face. Rex Henry would be gone, and then so would he. Somehow, it would all be for Emmett, and that was a beautiful notion. Delta Bohannon got that bit wrong, didn't she?

But he chose to remain ignorant of the date, the hour.

October yielded sunflowers more than ever, and so Emmett was outdoors for much of the day. He'd thought he'd mapped every inch of the property, when he came to the edge of the orchard. One tree was close enough to the house that spoiled apples dropped from its limbs and onto the roof. He was astonished that he had not seen it before. He knelt and from far away, he thought he must look like a modern-day pagan, on hands and knees before a holy tree. But he was looking at the ground at its base. It was the size of a brick, flat concrete embedded in the soil, and crudely lettered:

LITTLE EMMET

He brought Rex Henry out and pointed to it. Emmett could not speak, for his jaw would not unhinge. His finger twitched and dripped; he'd bitten the ham of his hand when the world became a blur. *Is this where I will be laid to rest?* He was Ebenezer Scrooge, Rex Henry the Ghost of Christmas Yet to Come. His leg was damp, the urine thick and hot as it pearled in the hairs.

Rex Henry moved quickly. Emmett could not see what he'd done, what he might do. In a moment, he was on the ground and Rex Henry was painting his face with cold water from the hose.

"You can't jump at every little thing," Rex Henry said. "Maybe when you've calmed down, you'll take another look."

For a full minute, Emmett sat with his hands pressed into his eyes. When he took them away, he watched the dime-sized orbs burst and fade as his mind and vision cleared. Then he looked.

And he wanted to laugh. The little marker didn't

say Emmet, at all. It read, *LITTLE EMINENT.* Beneath that, a date: *1925-1955.* At least it wasn't him.

"My dog," Rex Henry said. He patted the marker, picked at the vegetation that grew in the lettering.

Emmett quickly did the math. A thirty-year-old dog. His mother's beagle was twelve, and Aunt Jewel said she was on her last legs.

"I don't believe it," he said.

"Bluey the cattle dog lived to be twenty-nine. It's possible." Rex Henry had *The Guinness Book of World Records.*

"What kind of dog?"

"A mutt. Made up of all manner of things."

"What kind of dog?"

"Like the dog we saw."

"Just like that dog?"

"Yes. Just like that dog."

Emmett pressed on, "It also had stumpy little legs?"

"Yes."

"It was also long, like a hotdog?"

"Yes. Just like that."

Emmett thought of the trick Mr. Selmon, his Eufaula schoolteacher, had used to out the kids who hadn't done the reading. *What do you think Miss Havisham's parrot symbolizes? Damned fool, there never was a blessed parrot.* "Did it also have brown eyes?"

"What're you talking about? That funny-looking dog?" Rex Henry's face went sharp. "That dog's eyes were blue. Common in a merle dog. I'd have thought you'd noticed. This one's eyes were green."

They sat there, gnomish among the apples that littered the grass. Though Emmett could do little else but study his toes, he knew that Rex Henry was looking at him, as directly into his eyes as he could from that angle. Time passed. The skies yellowed, then bled.

Rex Henry stood. "Well. If ever you're ready to talk to me again, I'll be indoors."

"Okay."

"All right, then." And the lights glowed from the kitchen, the radio going, *"Hay-lo, everybody, hay-lo!"*

Emmett linked his arms and tucked them beneath his knees. He thought, *You are driving a bus. You are driving a bus. You are driving a bus.*

He skipped supper and went directly to his own cot. In the night, of all those in their hundreds, he had another nightmare. This one featured himself before a small audience, five or six people who sat in folding chairs. Emmett was naked, but this was not unusual; it was the odor he gave, like that of roses, but it had a sharpness to it, almost tawdry, like cheap perfume. He could not move as they came closer to smell him and smell him and smell him.

He came to Rex Henry and asked, "May I stay with you?," for he could not bear to be alone.

In Rex Henry's bed, he was absorbed, and was glad to abandon himself, if only until sunup.

The bus driver's eyes are green.

LOS OJOS Y LOS MANOS

A little after the New Year, there was a knock at the door.

Rex Henry answered and looked the girl up and down. "May I help you, miss?"

The girl rocked on her heels, craned her eyes around his shoulder, his neck. "Hi there. I'm looking for, I think he's your—I don't know, the boy who lives with you. Emmett."

Here was Rex Henry, blinking behind his spectacles.

Then the girl smiled. "Well, hey. There he is." And she rippled her fingers.

And there was Emmett, coming a bit too

quickly from the kitchen. He was going pink. His lips looked full and flushed, his eyes wide and watery. He made as if to wave back, but knotted his hand into a fist before he could.

Rex Henry gave a tight semblance of a smile and said, "Emmett has homework."

The girl frowned. "But he's not in school—"

"Good afternoon."

Emmett sat on the other side of the door until he could imagine the girl going up the walk to her own house, going inside, and locking the door behind her.

She'd been leaving school.

He'd slipped out of the house while no one was looking.

She'd been wearing a black straight skirt and a lavender turtleneck. She carried her shoes in one hand, her books in the other.

He'd been sitting on the bench outside the general store. He wore a flannel shirt with the collar unbuttoned, and there was something sweet that came off him that made her think of a boy genius. He sipped from a bottle of Big Red and she inhaled the sugar of it from where she stood as he exhaled the fumes of his cigarette. He'd been watching her go by for weeks.

What makes the difference between a thing that is quiet and a thing that is ordinary?

She'd been going forward down the road. When she thought he'd missed her, he'd called.

"What's your name?"

She told him. "Magical."

"I don't believe you."

"I never said you had to. But that's what it says on my driver's license." The girl called Magical snickered. Her features were sharp and her hair was short as a boy's.

"Where you heading to?"

She was going home, she said.

"From school?"

She told him, "Yes."

"At this time of day?" It was getting on for five o'clock, after all. "You get detention, or something?"

She smiled. "Saint Joan."

"How's that?"

"It's a play."

The boy took another swallow of red cream, and his lips were stained sweetly pink. "You the star?"

She was costume crew, she told him. "I do Saint Joan's hair." The play's leading lady, varsity track golden girl Diana Brownell, had long auburn locks that took about an hour to comb, brush, braid, pin, knot, and spray to the crown of her head. "They shaved Saint Joan's head in real life."

"Yeah, I heard that." The boy drained his cold drink and eased to his feet. "She was the one they burned, right?"

"That's her."

"Sad," he uttered. He was much taller on his feet than Magical had expected. She'd anticipated a small, stringy fellow of the sort she knew from the play's lighting crew, but here this one was, likely six-and-a-half feet and looked to be made of wire.

She licked her lower lip. "I don't think I caught your name?"

"Okay." He blinked, like a man startled. "Okay."

"Your name is Okay?"

He smiled, a queer, upside-down frown. "It's Emmett."

"Emmett Okay?"

"Sure."

"Is that your name?"

"No. Emmett is, not Okay."

"Well. That's okay, then." Magical hadn't given her last name either, so fair was fair.

"You going straight home?"

Magical said that she'd planned to go the long way. In truth, there was no long way, as the house where she lived with her grandmother was about a minute down the road. She figured, if he asked, that she might take him on a loop, up the highway and through Vanderpool's Paint and Body scrap yard, where there were auto carcasses as far as the eye could see. She mentioned the part about the scrap yard, her voice going low.

Emmett nodded, his Adam's apple bobbing, and he went quiet, looking into the empty Big Red bottle. He seemed, at that moment, to have cut himself away from this, Magical's, world. At the bottom of the bottle a gnat squirmed and buzzed in the sticky pink.

It looked as though that was that.

She'd never had to ask a boy to come with her before.

In school, they were always saying it was girls who were easy. That was dead wrong, for in her experience, it was the boys who were the easy ones. She'd never known a girl to go limp and drooling the way a boy did for just one glance. You could make a boy do anything. It was like hypnosis. And now, with mild discomfort, Magical was coming around to how it must feel. It was hell to leave a loose end; it made you feel as though you were not, and never were as potent as you thought.

"You doing anything right now?" she asked.

Emmett shrugged. "Not too much. As you can tell." That queer frown that was a smile.

"Well, then—" Granny Blanchefleur had a lot of sayings. Your body is a leaky vessel. Let the boy do the chasing. Don't come on too strong. Think how you'll look. Have poise. "—I'll just come out and say it. I want to take you out."

Emmett blinked. "Take me out?" Had she been watching him, too?

"Sure."

"To do what?"

"To do whatever."

"Well. All right."

"You'll come?"

"Why not?"

They set off up the highway, where they mounted a hill that dropped off into a panorama of grass and live oaks and lavender smears in the twilight. A Chevy pickup approached them from behind, headlights glowing so that Magical's shadow joined with Emmett's along the pavement, two heads and one arm each. Siamese sweethearts. And, perhaps prompted by their conjoined shadows, he drew closer to link his arm with hers. Because of his height, it was at an awkward angle, causing Magical to stumble and laugh. Their hips bumped together.

The pickup slowed to a chug, its window open and trailing the refrain of a slow song, *I fall in love too easily*. And it sped away when Magical turned back to look.

"Jeezus," she coughed.

Emmett offered his hankie, a piece of flannel, really, green and clean. She wondered if he'd snipped it from the tail of an old shirt. Granny Blanchefleur did that, made hankies and potholders and foul rags from the dresses she'd grown too fat for. It was a smart thing to do, very economical.

And it was soft against Magical's lips. "You like your things clean, don't you? I could smell the soap all the way from the street when I saw you."

"I like the Laundromat."

"You hang out there? I've never seen you."

"Only once in a blue moon. Washing stuff in the sink is quicker."

"I guess so." Not that she meant to, but her lips left a bloom of burgundy against the green.

At the bottom of the hill, a light went on in the little house where Magical lived with her grandmother. They had a little fenced-in patch where they grew peppers and squash, tomatoes on tripods made from old TV antennae. Their cat, Manuel, liked to roost beneath the tomatoes, where he could absorb the sun, but not too much. Now and then, when she weeded, Magical would come across trophies from Manuel's expeditions beyond the yard, tiny skulls, little splinters of bone from some doomed rodent half-buried between the rows of vegetables.

Out of respect (for Manuel, not for the dead), she left them where they were.

"Come on," she said; she didn't know why she was whispering. "Up this way."

She led Emmett across the highway, to a turn-off lined with auto parts. A sign, carved from cedar and varnished, read, VANDERPOOL'S PAINT & BODY. YOUR WAY: THE RIGHT WAY. She let her hand drop, and her finger looped around his belt. He did not protest this, and she did not ask if she was being too forward.

Then Emmett asked, "What's your favorite color?"

Magical kept forward, puzzled though she was. "Huh. Well. Green, I guess."

"Favorite animal?"

"Cats are pretty neat."

"Favorite thing to eat?"

"I like a lot of things."

"Favorite thing to read?"

She recalled the books assigned throughout the schoolyears. She really read maybe four of them. "Frankenstein was all right. Why? What's yours?" No one before had thought to ask.

"Mine?"

"Color, animal, all that."

Again, the mild puzzlement, now from him. Had no one thought to ask you, either?

"No favorite color."

"You must have just one."

"Nope."

"Favorite animal?"

"I like them all."

"So, that probably means you're a vegetarian?" Magical had never met a vegetarian before. She assumed they all lived in queer, congested places like San Francisco.

"No, I'm not."

"You like all animals and you still eat meat?"

"Yup. That's not so funny."

"Yeah?"

"No." His face gathered inward, on edge. "It's not."

Magical swallowed, and she felt herself beginning a slow descent into submission, which, though unfamiliar, she did not resist. For once, she wanted to see what might happen.

And now here was Emmett, leading her up the road. The auto parts thickened from the odd cluster of fenders and tires to entire vehicles, just a few, before multiplying into neat rows of pickups, Chevrolets and Fords, then lumpy Pontiacs in succulent jewel tones.

Magical chuckled. "Now would be a good time to have a favorite color."

"I don't have one."

"You're not color blind, or something, are you?"

"I don't think so."

"So, pick a color."

"Well. All right—" Keeping his left arm (somehow, this seemed to be his good arm) looped through hers, Emmett extended his free fist and let one finger spring from it. "That one."

Magical squinted. "That's green." A Pontiac the color of an emerald; it backed up to the row of

Chevrolets. "You didn't pick that one just for me, did you?"

"I guess I did."

They got in, she the driver, he the passenger. They did not touch each other the night through, save for now and then linking their fingers into a common web. They seemed eager to prolong whatever it was they had as much as they could. Magical told him about her Granny Blanchefleur, stories she'd told Magical about her youth in Epsom Downs ("That's in England, where they have the big horse race. The queen goes and everything."), the fair at which she'd met her man and come to these Hills a bride of sixteen. Grandma was called Blanchefleur, Mother, long dead, was called Zelie, Daughter was called Magical; they sounded like a family of witches. And it was true that Granny read palms for extra pocket money. Emmett told her about his Aunt Jewel, who also read palms.

Magical asked, "Is that who you live with?"

"Not anymore. I live with a man now."

"A man."

Emmett propped his feet on the dashboard. "That's right." But he seemed unsure, now that he was saying the word again.

Magical thought it unwise to press him, not

there, not yet. Instead, she unrolled the window a bit more to let the smoke from their cigarette escape. She passed the butt to him. "So."

"So what?"

"How long were you watching me?"

At this, he smiled, a true one that caused the lines around his eyes to pull upward. "A while."

"I only see you in that one place. Always at the same time. When I see you."

"It's when I can get out."

Between half-three and five o'clock was when Rex Henry liked to lie down for an hour or two. At first, Emmett read or wandered unclothed along the one hundred acres, but the routine had become too much for him. It was hard to say how. And so, he decided to dress and go for a walk, nowhere special, not far, until he realized that he was standing before Vera at the general store in town, buying a Big Red. He made a habit of this, the minute Rex Henry put head to pillow. He would sit on the steps outside the general store and sip from his Big Red. He would not articulate the words, not even in his mind, that it was quite a relief to be on his own again. No worrying. No watching. No worship. And he began to think how fine he looked in clothes.

He had thought the first time that Rex Henry

had heard him, for he'd come back as soon as Rex Henry had roused.

"Where're you off to?"

Emmett heard himself say, "Just got back."

"Back from where?" Rex Henry knew; he just wanted to hear it from the boy.

But without a beat, Emmett told Rex Henry that he'd been doing Renata's Walk, to get his mind clean. He didn't know what made him say it, for Rex Henry knew the number of hairs on his head. It was a matter of time before Rex Henry turned him out, and he braced himself for the great expulsion.

But, touch wood, it hadn't happened.

Rex Henry had eyed him, nodded, and dressed, each time.

Was this a recognition? Blessing for respite into the rude world?

Or was Rex Henry made of weaker stuff, after all?

He didn't question it; he would go mad if he did. Rex Henry went to sleep, and Emmett went out.

Now he sat beside a girl called Magical and shared a cigarette. He refused to feel contrition for it. Bacchanalia be blessed.

He asked her if she knew how to read palms.

She snorted. "No. It's a crock."

"No, it isn't. My Aunt Jewel does it. Did it. She told a lady who'd just turned fifty that she would have a baby."

"And did she?"

"She had twins that Christmas."

"Lucky guess for auntie."

"Well, I bet I could read yours." This was bold, untrue. Bacchanalia, too. But Emmett's world had grown and reduced itself to this car, all in a few minutes. He had room for nothing else. Besides, he thought in the back of his mind, it was something he knew and Rex Henry didn't, something he could reveal to him or not. And he swallowed the thought away.

Magical laughed, bit her lip. She took the butt from him and rippled the fingers on her free hand. "That's where you're tripping up already. Only chicks do those tricks."

"I can. I watched my Aunt Jewel enough, even when she told me to buzz off."

The girl sighed, putting on a big show, *I'm doing you such a grand favor.* Her palm unfurled against his knee; she was not like a flower.

He let the nail of his index finger trip along the

158

line that scored her palm straight across. He heard himself say that she would live to the age of one-hundred-and-thirty ("That's ten years older than the oldest woman."), she would live in a small house with many dogs ("And one cat…maybe two."), and she would do exactly what she wanted to do, when she wanted to do it.

Her color rose high and red. "You're making all that up."

Emmett shook his head. "No, I'm not." But he was smiling, too, and she knew that he knew that he was making it up, and it was all right. "It could happen."

And that was all right, because he knew that she knew that it could.

"Well." Rex Henry did not appear angry, not in any knowable sense of it. "We don't need to talk about that again, I don't think."

Emmett had not moved from his post by the door. He had not seen the girl go inside yet.

"But let me say this." Rex Henry descended a hand slowly upon Emmett's scalp, like ooze. It made the boy shiver with equal parts pleasure and fear, so much so that it hurt. "It is not the way you're meant to be."

Emmett looked up. "What?"

"Where she is, and where she's going—Can you picture yourself on her arm? Try it." Rex Henry's tone was not mocking. He said it gently, a little sadly.

Emmett had seen in her hands that she would live to do exactly what she wanted to do when she wanted to do it. He imagined this girl called Magical in her small house, anywhere, tending to a herd of twenty dogs. She would wake at dawn or at noon. She would eat as much or as little as she pleased. She would wear anything or nothing.

To Rex Henry's credit, Emmett did not see himself at her side.

He unhinged his jaw, to speak, to tell Rex Henry all, where he had seen her, the weeks, months in which he'd spent his time watching her from the steps outside the general store, how he had seen her before she had seen him. This last seemed the most important.

Rex Henry waved his hand. Of course. He already knew. But he did say, "Watch her."

Emmett let his head rest against the door.

"You can do that, can't you?" Rex Henry got to his feet. "Watch her?"

CONFITEOR

Magical John had long hair until the lice came. Granny Blanchefleur tried dunking her head in kerosene, but they came back, more ravenous than before. "Think of it this way," she'd said, shears in hand, "in a few weeks' time, you'll look like Falconetti." And Magical fingered the tufts like bristles over her skull. She dared herself to look at the dark tresses that wreathed the kitchen chair on which she sat. Her grandmother bound them with twine and placed them in the yard for the birds to make their nests.

The girl went to the little mirror in the bathroom. She looked like Falconetti already, as Joan of Arc before the burning.

Magical John had carried parasites before. When she was eight she had mites. When she was thirteen, hookworm. And every summer she played host to chiggers, but then, everyone did. This was her fifth encounter with lice. She had long ago accepted that she would never be clean, and let the earth's pests do what they wanted with her. Her grandmother had devised all manner of home remedies for flushing the girl of them, but until now, Magical had never worried much. Her pests were polite guests; they ate their fill and knew when to leave. If anything, she was healthier for it; while the others kept out of school for some little cough, Magical remained in the pink.

Things were different, now that she was older. Years passed and now she had gone from hookworms to boys. They couldn't help themselves—that's what they said. And Magical couldn't help herself—that's what she would have said, if the world really were the same place for her as for them. At fourteen, she'd touched herself and imagined someone touching her, day after day—until finally someone did. She didn't remember his name, Warren or William, a boy in her homeroom, they went to his place in Himmel Creek, where he and his five brothers slept in a bunkhouse.

She came away, as she did from that time on, all the healthier for that, too. She was pink and calm and felt that she would not need any sustenance but that blooming feeling again.

Now she thought. And she itched. She looked to make sure her grandmother wasn't watching her and gave herself one long scratch.

Warren/William and his brothers. The fellow who said hello at the Memorial Day parade. The one who operated the fireworks stand on the highway. Which of them was it?

She scratched and scratched. And it hurt to pee.

She thought darkly, *Which of you was it? Doesn't matter. Doesn't matter. You're all filthy.*

The blooming feeling had gone to rot.

Until now, she really had been in the pink of health.

"It's because you ate dirt when you were a baby," Granny Blanchefleur said. Outside the bathroom door, she swept up the smallest hairs. "And, little do you know, you still do. You get things garden-fresh, you're bound to swallow a peck of dirt. You used to be as clean as they come, because of all that."

Magical scraped at herself, above and below. She sat on the toilet and wept and burned. She was sure Granny Blanchefleur hadn't shaved her head just because of the lice. She didn't even know if she was pretty or not.

What was she to do?

Her grandmother told her to go to the drive-in. "Go now." It was only just two o'clock in the afternoon.

Go to the movies? Magical called through the door, "They're not open 'til it gets dark."

Granny Blanchefleur said again, "Go now."

"And do what?"

"Sit in Delta's car. You sit there and think. Maybe you'll straighten up and fly right. The Bohannon girl knew things. She had visions. She knew the bad of all that comes to—"

Magical couldn't take much more. She bleated, "You were fifteen when you did it."

Her grandmother reminded her that she'd been betrothed at the time. "And married not long after. Different story." She threw a headscarf at Magical, the one that doubled as a chapel veil.

The Fairlane was pearly and incorruptible. In the two months it sat in the drive-in's parking lot, neither damp nor dust nor dirt had laid a blemish. It was shiny as the day its owner, Delta Bohannon, parked it before the big screen. Everyone talked about Delta Bohannon as though she had always been, as though it were common knowledge to know of her. She disappeared, all but for her little toe. The drive-in's management offered to take in the dog that found it, just as they offered to preserve the Fairlane; the Bohannon family were too grief-stricken to say anything but Yes. The dog lived the life of a mascot now, keeping vigil at the passenger's door. People waited their turn to sit in the driver's seat, to meditate on their wrongs and the mysteries of this world and the next. *I believe in the forgiveness of sins, the resurrection of the body*, and whatnot. The drive-in's manager charged two dollars, much more than he did for regular admission.

And when Magical arrived, there was already a line.

"Ma'am?" A little girl in a red sweater, the hood pulled over her dark hair, held out a collection can. "Two dollars to sit, two-fifty for the dog to sit with you."

"How long?"

"Five minutes." The little girl rocked the can up and down so that the coins inside pinged and dinged.

Magical remembered, from where, she didn't know: *When a coin in the coffer rings, a soul from Limbo springs.* Maybe it was from a game show. She dug through her change purse until she found the silver dollar and change Granny had given her. She could have skipped the drive-in and gone to the indoor theater in Andermatt. She could have skipped town and changed her name to Maria Falconetti.

But her grandmother would know. She studied the women's faces up and down the line, recognizing in some the shape of a nose, big hands, narrow jawlines, pieces of the boys whom she, Magical John, had fed off of.

She could smell herself.

She asked the little hooded girl if Delta Bohannon wasn't that dingbat who sat in front every Saturday night and talked to herself. Magical had been here before; when she was not devouring her date, she could see the pearly Fairlane before the big screen, and hear the nonsense that wafted through its open window. Delta Bohannon was mad. Now that she was dead, was she suddenly a paragon? Magical hadn't realized she'd been talking until she caught herself saying, "If she'd lived another fifty years, I tell you what, she'd be shitting her pants in some nuthatch and we wouldn't give a damn about her."

The little girl pulled her hood over her eyes.

The woman two heads in front of Magical turned and said, *"And why beholdest thou the mote that is in thy sister's eye, but considerest not the beam that is in thine own eye?"* She swallowed and went on, before turning back around. "A little bit of grace goes a long way, missy."

Magical sighed. She itched and she could not scratch. She was sure the woman would turn just in time to catch her. She told the little girl, "I'll sit with the dog." Two more quarters made two-fifty.

The car was clean and, though it did not run, its radio worked and was tuned in to Oral Roberts. Magical changed the station, leaping from place to place until she settled on Chet Baker. She let the dog rest her head against her shoulder and tried to make the most of her five minutes, a good doze. The chapel veil drooped around her shoulders. To the car's credit, Magical did not itch. She did not think of that, or her grandmother, or the mothers outside who knew what she'd been doing with their sons. Not even the notion that crept up more and more frequently now, *I fall in love too easily...*

Then came a *Bang! Bang! Bang!* Against her head and Magical woke. The little girl in the red hood had come a-knocking. "Folks're waiting on you, lady," she called.

VESPERS

The girl came to the house, but Emmett would not let her in. Instead, he took her out, like a real beau. And Rex Henry let him, though Emmett would catch sight of the Chevrolet pickup, no matter where they went. These were spur of the moment decisions, made when Emmett had thought they were far out of anyone's earshot: "Let's go to the Rock Shop. Let's go to the library."

They hid out in the newspaper section, because it had the plushest chairs. They read all the horoscopes they could find, and the personals. Emmett especially liked it when Magical would read to him the Missed Connection ads, doing all the voices.

"To a handsome fella I saw at Blue Jean's last Fri. I was the one who did the grapefruit trick, tall, curvy and blond. I'll be there tonite, the gal with the grapefruit."

"Saw you at the drugstore. Thought you were UNFORGETTABLE. You wore a pair of great heels and had a great smile. I rang you up and we talked beekeeping for a while. Hope you come my way again."

The librarian asked, "Shouldn't you two be in school?"

Magical giggled. "It's a professional development day."

"That so?"

"Yes, ma'am."

Luckily for Magical and Emmett, it was—as the librarian found when she called the administrative office at Phillip D. Andermatt High School. She told them, "If you're going to hang around here all afternoon, you might try doing something constructive with your time." And she directed Magical and Emmett to the tables and covered its top with newspapers.

"Well, all right," Magical snickered.

"What's going on in the world today?" Emmett asked. He scooted from his place across the table to sit beside Magical, as soon as the librarian left her desk.

"Same ol', same ol'."

But Emmett browsed, nonetheless. He came across an ad for Delta Bohannon's car, not for sale, but for admission, right there in the drive-in lot. He pointed it out to Magical. She scoffed. "I got to sit in it. Everyone's lining up like it's Disney Land."

"Is the dog still there?"

Magical blinked. "Yes, she's still there."

"Do they treat her right? She's a good dog. Do they treat her right?"

"Well, yes, I believe so. She looked fine when I was there."

"Okay."

"What's wrong? You're sweating and all."

"I'm fine." Emmett mopped at his brow and recognized that his shirt, now damp, chilled him.

Magical squeezed his shoulder. "You sure?"

"Yes."

"You want to do something else?"

Emmett swallowed and swallowed. He balled his hands, for he would not bite. He considered sitting on his hands, but this would not do, either.

Magical asked again, taking one of his hands in hers, "You want to do something else?"

They took a moment to breathe. Then

Emmett sipped tentatively at the air and led her out.

"Boy!" Magical laughed out loud, her delight sudden and tangible; Emmett was rocked by it. It had been a long walk from town and he was afraid that she would be too vexed to care. "I haven't been here in ages. Not since my sixth birthday."

On account of this Indian summer, the funfair remained open throughout the fall. The merry-go-round glittered, the loudspeakers piped Judy Garland singing "Boys and Girls Like You and Me." The concession offered apple turnovers, icing striped and wonderfully sticky. "It's funny," Magical said around a bite, "I go this way all the time, you know, just on errands and what have you. And I always thought they tore this place down."

"It's only open in the summer, usually," Emmett said.

"Even then. Even then, I didn't notice it."

Since Emmett had last visited, the funfair added a petting zoo. It was not much more than a few goats penned in with two very uppity-looking alpacas that kept to themselves. There were gumball machines that were filled with fodder. Emmett let one of the goats kiss his chin, his nose, his ears. Magical laughed; she'd forgotten how badly she itched. They fed the creatures from their palms and even the alpacas could be persuaded to drift over.

The lady at the concession called out, "That's love. Right there, that's love."

Aside from her, there was no one else around, no one to watch them. Emmett would never admit to how easily he could breathe now.

Magical and me. No one else.

Did he love her? If he did, here was a different breed of what he felt for Rex Henry. There, Emmett was not for himself, body and soul given over to a pair of divine hands. And part of him relished this. He adored being shaped. He burrowed himself into Rex Henry and felt his weight being cradled, his mind suspended. When he says JUMP, I'll ask HOW HIGH?

Magical would not ask that of him. And that made him think highly of her.

This was her world as much as anyone's, Emmett could see that. She did not live for anyone, just as she would not die for anyone. Perhaps she really would live to one-hundred-and-thirty, because she wanted to.

Boys and girls, like you and me…

She poked him. Her headscarf had been wrested away, the dark tufts underneath spiky with the highway breeze. "Let's get on the merry-go-round."

Emmett shook his head: That was for him and Rex Henry. A grave disloyalty. *I will have no other gods before you.* "Let's ride the mule."

She took the reins, Emmett the rear, his hands cupping her shoulders. They circled the tiny corral a hundred times. Magical suggested that they close their eyes, all the better to imagine that they were really going somewhere. Emmett took the opportunity to smell her, and her essence was not of perfume; hers was a yeasty aroma, all body, like his. He'd always thought he smelled bad, and that no amount of bathing could erase it. Now he smelled himself on another, and it was not putrid. It was so good he wanted to eat it.

He buried his face into the crook of her neck. And she rested her head against his, eyes still closed. He saw nothing of the world but Rex Henry's Chevrolet, parked across the road, however long it had been there—and not even that put him at sixes and sevens. The mule went around and around the tiny corral, and when their fifteen minutes were up, they paid to go again. And again, and again, and again.

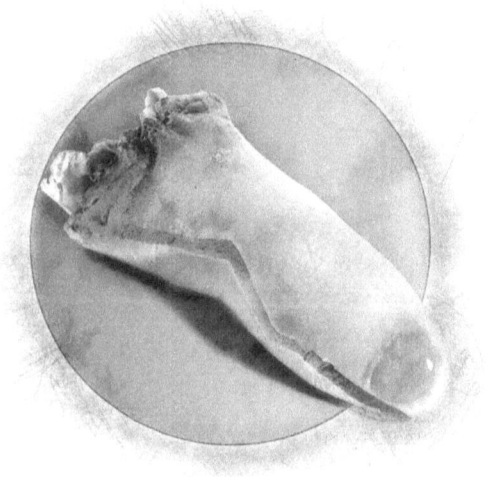

LA TEMPESTA ASCOSA

The highway wind went on, a real torrent. Cars up and down the road for a mile. It was enough to carry the trash from the funfair to the little knot of people across the way.

These were not devotees, but real people. Ivo and Laura Ansky stood on rickety legs, squinting against the sounds of the rude world. They clung to each other and could not quite look anyone else in the eye. They, as those who have awoken from an enchantment, were rousing from their mourning in which anger dominated above all else. Beside them, just as incensed, also gripping at one another, were Dennis and Rose Bohannon. They had visited with one another, after hearing of their losses. They knew what had happened and now, after coffee hours and cake and dinners and days in which the sun rose and set over talks that mapped out where Renata had been, and where Delta had been and how no man, no matter how virtuous, never just vanishes, body and soul, they all awoke together. The romance had gone and the hardness of it remained: "Our babies are gone."

They called the law.

The law's first order of business was to chase away the devotees, and there were a lot of them. The faithful were indignant. A woman shouted, "The Lord will come on His day and judge the lot of you!"

The law came closer and said, "Well, today's only Wednesday. Now, get on out of here. Go on." The faithful backed away, tight-limbed and tight-lipped.

That done, the law scoured the cedar woods.

"We have something," they said.

"God," Rose Bohannon said, a curse more than an invocation. "I painted that toe." And she moved to take it from the policeman's hand, but he pulled it from her reach.

"We'll need this," he said.

The nail was painted pink, Cutex Robins and Roses. Here was Delta Bohannon's foot in her mother's lap, mother and daughter sitting cross-legged on the window seat, and all was pink and soft. Delta laughed and Mother did, too, to keep her daughter company.

"God," she said again. Then, full of fury, heavily, "GOD." She searched the surrounding faces wildly for something on which to exercise her rage. There were the Anskys, her husband, the multi-headed body of the law.

She balled her fists, emitted a sound that fell somewhere between a growl and a roar.

Then she charged.

Dennis Bohannon was close behind, "Rose-ba-by, Rose-baby, don't—"

The man she caught submitted to her abuses. He did not shield his eyes when her claws came at him and seemed to relish the scratches.

Dennis Bohannon lifted her away, her toes grazing the thin grass, having lost her shoes. The law crept nearer, but did not approach them outright. "Okay now," he panted. He wrested her against him when she tried to turn loose. "Okay now. That's all."

"I WANT HIM OUT OF HERE."

The man, small and spry like a goblin, knelt, swaying. He did not move to the Chevrolet pickup, nor did he try to get up. His eyes fogged, like

181

someone in the throes of passion.

"Rose-baby—"

"GET HIM OUT." Rose Bohannon wrenched free and made enough time to dive and bite the little man's cheek. She roared in his face, "YOU HEAR ME, YOU LEECH? YOU RATFUCK. GET OUT. PICK UP YOUR NASTY RAT-FUCK TAIL AND GET OUT."

After a minute or so of this, the little man did get up. He brushed his old corduroys of dust and grass. He turned and he did not go to the Chevrolet pickup in which he'd arrived. He looked first to the funfair across the road (Ivo and Laura Ansky, for a moment, saw Renata leading the mule by the reins in the corral). Then, he went down the road, and he limned the edge of it in slow, even steps.

Rose Bohannon howled, "YOU RATFUCK."

Dennis Bohannon eased her away, ready to carry her. "That's it now. That is it."

Ivo and Laura Ansky were ready to watch the little man until he disappeared. He grew smaller and smaller against the wavering line of heat between ground and sky. And, as if drawn by soul not sight, he swerved, into the tall grass, stumbling and dropping to his knees at the purple plywood cross that loomed out of the earth.

The law brought their heads together. Without words, they communicated amongst themselves: "Watch him."

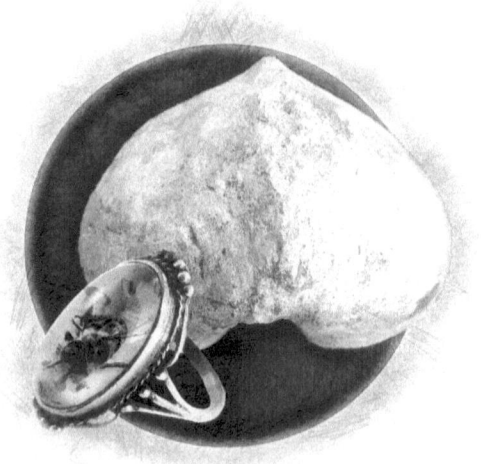

FOUR BITS

Emmett had a dream in which he was digging. In the dream, he was a dog, but he still had his long arms and fingers. With them, he dug. He paused to look up and, lo, he was in Rex Henry's yard. A light was on in the house and a window opened. His Aunt Jennie poked her head out and said, "Who's my boy? You-hoo, that's who—"

When Emmett woke, he peered outside, then crept to the edge of the yard, to the base of the apple tree. The ground was smooth and undisturbed. The Little Eminent marker was still in place.

In life, his Aunt Jennie had never sounded so perky.

Later, in Rex Henry's bed, he said, "I think I'm

an animal."

"Well." Rex Henry nodded against the pillow they shared, and he looked very sage, putting Emmett at ease. "That's what you are, then. Does that bother you?"

It took Emmett a minute to chew over those words. He played them again in his head and caught a sourness this time around. His Aunt Jennie had sounded like that. *No man's going to touch me again. But you'll do.* It bent him so badly he hated her, and yet he would do anything she wanted.

Now Rex Henry asked again, "Does that bother you?"

Emmett felt himself bending and murmured, "I don't know."

Magical John came to the house again. She stood outside knocking while Emmett and Rex Henry sat in the kitchen and talked.

Emmett said, "No."

Rex Henry sat back, folded his arms. "No?"

And Emmett said again, "No."

"You don't want to?"

"I don't think I can."

"So, you do want to?"

"I don't know."

Rex Henry shook his head, almost sorrowfully. He smeared his toast with margarine. "You'll have to come up with something other than *I don't know*, one of these days."

This made Emmett's toes curl. *I don't know* was a perfectly good answer to things you hadn't the answers to. Why say *Yes* or *No* when you didn't even know both sides of the thing?

All the while, Magical knocked and knocked and knocked. Emmett could smell her through the door. She hollered, "Hell-oooo? Y'all alive in there?" Then she drummed a little rhythm, shave-and-a-haircut-two-bits.

Rex Henry scowled her way. But he did not seem disapproving. He did not seem taken with her, either. He had only said to watch her.

Shave-and-a-haircut-two-bits.

"So," Rex Henry said over the din. "What's the deal?"

"Don't you know?" Emmett had thought Rex Henry couldn't have heard him, but who was he kidding?

From outside, "Emmett Anhalt, Emmett An-halt, c'mon out and play…"

Rex Henry crunched his toast, white bread,

enriched. *Who told thee that thou wast naked?*

"…it's Magical, it's Magical, and she won't wait all day."

And Emmett wept. It had been ages since he had done so, and he'd been hoping to save it for a moment alone. And now it all came forth in an awful rush. His face swelled, and he thought his eyes might grow heavy enough to fall out. But he did not utter a sound, did not say a word. He let his breath come in long hisses between his teeth. This was the moment at which he felt that he might truly be an animal, after all, impotent and mute and dirty and saved only by how pitiful he could make himself.

"You have my blessing," Rex Henry said, at last, "if that's what you were looking for."

Emmett snuffled.

"I suppose there's worse things you could be doing with your spare time."

Emmett nodded.

"A boy ought to have a girl. That's how it ought to be."

Emmett nodded again, unsure this time. And, like that, he saw the rift between them, the divide laid down by Rex Henry. The relief came and he did not know if he wanted it. *Let me stay, let me stay with you.* He felt his own mortality creep across his chest as shadows crept across the kitchen walls. Where was the safety of Rex Henry's bed, the clean sheets?

Shave-and-a-haircut-two-bits.

Rex Henry smiled, and relieved Emmett of his burdens, for the time. "Go on. Enjoy yourself."

"You think she's the girl?"

"For you? Yes."

"For the long haul?"

"As long as it's meant to be."

Emmett turned in the doorway. "How long is that?"

Rex Henry thought. "About a year." He studied the grooves in the ceiling's woodwork, the one that was shaped like a man in sunglasses. He nodded, as if he had it in confidence from that shape. "Yes. About one year."

Emmett grew chilled. He might well have asked that question, the one he could not ask: *When will I die?* It all seemed tied together. Had Renata Ansky known, or Delta Bohannon? They had accepted their time, their joy and horror, with grace. And so must he. "All right," he sighed, and he got up to go.

Rex Henry rapped on the tabletop. "Now, hold on."

"What?"

"You'll be back by supper."

"Yes."

"And there will be no going out after."

"All right."

"I want you to see something."

Emmett rocked on his heels. "What is it?"

"I want you to see, first. See what you think."

Emmett knew before Rex Henry could say more. A new girl, a new and blessed girl. The thrill of it rose to his brain where it burst and, disappointingly, evaporated. How many blessed and venerable and virtuous persons did the world make? They all seemed to crop up from everywhere, like chiggers in the grass. It made Emmett wonder at his own goodness of heart; what all had he done so far, and what all could he do to become venerable? Was it the same for boys? Would he live long enough to do good? Many of the blessed, it seemed, met their end before their twenty-first birthday. These were the ones people remembered, at least.

And this seemed, all at once, more important than what you could do. You could do nothing and everyone would love you anyway.

He brought this up to Magical at the Rock

Shop, censoring much of it. He quoted something Rex Henry had said of Renata and Delta: "Whom the gods love, dies young.'"

Magical, who had been listening respectfully, picked up her straw, tore the paper from its end, and blew the rest of the wrapper into Emmett's face. If it were anyone else (even Rex Henry, he found himself thinking), Emmett would have been angry. Instead, he let the corners of his mouth move.

"You're talking about being famous, right?" she asked.

He nodded.

Her hair had grown into a spiky cap over her head. She did not look like a boy anymore, but she did not look yet like a girl. "Aren't you supposed to do something to get famous?"

"Well—"

"Like invent the lightbulb, or write a great poem? If you die and get famous, but you didn't do anything, that's like getting a prize for being pretty. Or because someone felt sorry for you." Magical dipped an onion ring into a puddle of ketchup. "Even if a person has a good idea and just wants to tell other people about it, it's okay if he's famous."

"Like Jesus?"

"Sure. And others. Who wants to go around

like a goody-goody and then die? Okay, Little Miss So-And-So was ever so good. She didn't do anything. Who cares?"

Emmett wanted to tell her that she was missing the point, futile though it seemed. He said it anyway. "Lots of people do. People remember them for how they were. And how they died for it."

Magical picked the crust from around her onion ring, loosed the worm inside. "You a papist?"

Emmett thought. "No." He and Rex Henry seemed higher than any ecclesia.

"A flagellant?"

"What's that?"

"Where you hit yourself," she said, "to cleanse your sins. That's what they say, anyway. I think anyone who does that gets some kind of fun from it. And it's all right. Nothing wrong with it. So long as you don't knock anyone's lights out."

Emmett didn't think it was fun. While he had never struck himself, the gnashing of his teeth, the rendering of his skin, he did not pretend that it didn't hurt. It was not pleasurable, but it relieved him of whatever it was that crawled inside. "No one does that."

"I ought to take you to a tent revival. You'd see." Magical remembered that William/Warren and his brothers were tent revivalists. All those switches they kept beneath their bunks; it made sense.

Emmett shook his head. "Not like that."

Magical let the onion worm alone. She put out her hands, palms up, on the tabletop. She did not take his hands, nor did she ask him to take hers. Her hands were there, should he need them.

He gave himself over.

Her fingers were half the length of his and smooth. Emmett was willing to bet that she'd never even bitten her nails.

Magical began, slow, "When you get like this—" she paused to scoot her chair to the side for a little boy in cowboy boots, "—what do you do?"

He shrugged. His hands were ridged, up and down, rough terrain from thumb to wrist.

"You ever try and just think of nice things?" Magical turned away, shied pink.

That was an easy one. Emmett had Rex Henry to thank for that. "I think about Paradise," he said.

"All right. That's something good." She squeezed his thumb. "What's it like?"

Again, that was easy. "Like where I took you."

"What, the funfair?"

"Yes. Just like that."

They sat, their arms a bridge across the table, and both absorbed memories, new and old, shared and private, of that place. Apple turnovers and cajeta. Merry-go-rounds. Goats and mules. Not too hot, not too cool. Live oaks. The railroad and the grass. Boys and girls like you and me. Magical had had her sixth birthday party there. Emmett saw it before he came, a hundred times from the Chevrolet, from the road, from his mind's eye in Eufaula. It was a good place.

"What's nice about it," Magical said, "is we can go whenever we want."

"You have to have money to go." Rex Henry gave Emmett an allowance, fifty cents a week, which he sometimes withheld if he was displeased. Emmett would never know what it was he had or hadn't done; Rex Henry would eye him and say, "You know." And so, on those occasions, Paradise seemed far away.

Magical leaned back in her chair and looked at him, making little faces at him until he smiled. "Well. They lock the gate at six—," it was more of a chain-link fence, really, "—but it's not like they have a guard dog or anything."

For that, Emmett put the last of his spending money toward a little silver ring for her, set with an amber. It fit on her smallest finger.

Magical couldn't say anything, save to remark,

"There's a cute little bug in it." She couldn't tell if it was a fly or a bee. She decided that it ought to be a bee, for who would make jewelry out of a preserved housefly? She surveyed the Rock Shop's gifts, the affordable things. There were earrings of shark teeth and pennants of fossilized scorpions. There were petrified gastropods, for this part of the world had once been the floor of a great ocean. Finally, she lit on something. It was seventy-five cents, and it would say what she meant without being too forward.

"The cowboy heart," she told the fellow behind the desk, who brought it out from its glass case and dropped it into a paper sack.

"One prehistoric clam," the fellow said and handed it to her with a little flourish.

It fit in Emmett's palm. It was the size of a golf ball, and you could still see the ripples in its shell. "It's pretty," he murmured. What else could he say? *I love you* was not right, not yet. She was too solid for that. To love her would be to love himself.

But it coursed between them, as nourishment from a mother to her unborn child.

Magical tugged his sleeve. "Come on," she said and led him into the moving dark outside.

It was ten minutes to six.

HOPE MAKETH NOT ASHAMED

At that hour, LaRue Martin took confession at Saint Ossana of Mantua.

"It's been about a week since last time," she told the screen.

On the other side, the man of the cloth stirred. The cupboard was narrow, and any movement was felt throughout. "I remember."

She launched into it. "I'm impatient. I want it to happen so badly."

"It's a long engagement. As it ought to be. You want to be sure, don't you?"

"Supposing I'm sure now?" She shifted her weight on the bench from one knee to the other.

"I'm sure you heard your mother say this: Marriage is a marathon, not a race."

"All right, but how long do people usually wait?" The girl sighed. "Maybe I ought to be talking about this to a girl—but girls who'll know what I'm on about are pretty few and far between."

"You have—what is it, one more year at the high school?"

"Yes."

The man of the cloth swallowed, then sneezed into his sleeve. The force of it carried through the screen. "Excuse me. The point is, you've got time."

"Too much of it. I want him now."

"Well, let's not be greedy—" the man of the cloth chuckled, "—you can see the irony, seeing as how much you'd be giving up."

"I know. But it hurts."

"It's one day at a time. You've got one year left at the high school. Think of your studies, activities—what all do you do for extracurriculars?"

"I'm shooting guard for the Lady Rams—that's our basketball team—"

"Good."

"—and I'm on the yearbook. I'm a soprano in the choir. And I'm on the cotillion decoration committee."

"How grand. You've got a dress all picked out?"

"Yes. It's got a velvet bodice and a tulle skirt, very simple, black and white."

"Sounds like Grace Kelly. And a date? Who's the lucky fellow?"

"I was going to go by myself…"

"Now. There must be some nice fellow around."

"Well, there's Jesse Gipson. He's been buzzing around a lot."

The cupboard creaked as the man of the cloth nodded. "Well, there you go. Jesse Gipson. Is he a nice fellow?"

"Very."

"Good looking?"

"In a duck's ass kind of way, sure." Another creak, top to bottom, as LaRue Martin adjusted her chapel veil. "I'm sorry, that was rude of me."

"I'll let that one slide."

"Thank you."

"The point is to enjoy the time you have. Don't go rushing ahead. And I know as well as you, it's all very romantic. But I said it once, and I'll say it again: Be sure. Always, you've got to be sure."

LaRue Martin picked at her nails. "I know it." She drew in the close air, slow, between the gap in her front teeth and held it until a tightness began in her breast. She savored it, as she savored all little hurts. Then she released it, feeling the color bleed back into her face. "Thank you. And my penance?"

"Say hey to Jesse Gipson for me. That's all."

"Sure?"

"You're a good girl. I trust you."

"Okay. Thanks again. And I'll tell Jesse you say hello."

"Here's some Romans for you, before you run off. *Patience, experience; and experience, hope: and hope maketh not ashamed.*"

She savored the words as she savored her tiny hurts, and she was gone.

The man of the cloth, Father Simon Kavka, thought that the call to God was something else for women than it was for men. For one thing, the women were allowed the ardor of it. Think of it—the most perfect man! The ceremony of a postulant's first vows was done in the manner of a wedding; girls bought white gowns, ordered bouquets. Their fathers gave them away. They were brides, and the Lord their husband. And, because this most perfect man was a lifetime away, the longing remained. A marriage that would never leave its honeymoon phase.

Just as he suspected, LaRue Martin, walking home, was thinking of Christ. Just as he suspected, she was thinking of Him the way other girls might think of James Dean. "That's how they get you," Simon Kavka said to himself. There never was a plain-looking Savior on any crucifix. And His beauty never faded. The convent at Elam held a branch of the biggest fan club the world had ever seen. The Sisters of Adoration, they were called, where the average age was thirty. They were young. They were starry-eyed. They were called.

Perhaps that was the best way. He'd heard husbands describe being drawn to their wives when they first met, and vice versa. It was something he could only nod to; love, the wildness of it, was something he had yet to experience. His was intellectual, familial, a few times physical. He was in the right business, no question, but he envied the Sisters and their talk. If he could be let to love... All the old sayings came at Simon Kavka: *You don't pick whom you love; it happens when you least expect it; love lives in cottages as well as in court...*

Jesse Gipson had a lot to live up to.

ANIMALS

They'd stood roadside by the Rock Shop, thumbs out, until a woman in a station wagon picked them up. "I thought they tore that place down," she'd remarked when they told her where they were going.

They'd jumped the chain-link fence.

They linked arms for, without the light of the sun, Paradise was dark and unfamiliar. The devotees began their road meditations earlier in the day now that it was cold and the highway empty. Emmett's eyes at night had always been keen, and so he led Magical around picnic tables and trashcans and benches. The silence of the place made them want to talk. Magical sang:

"Last night we strolled through the garbage,
Her greasy hand in mine,
Her clammy lips on the back of my neck,
Oh, life is so dee-vine!"

Then she stopped, held Emmett back. "Jesus," she breathed.

Emmett looked. "It's only a kitty."

"Just a kitty? Or a wildcat? I didn't even think about that."

"It's a kitty."

And a slinky shape leapt and skittered away. They waited a moment before a shriek rose from the goats' pen, then two. A scuffle followed, whispery hisses and low growls, a succession of wet panting, a pitty-pat as the beasts parted.

Magical poked Emmett and asked, "Kitties?"

"No."

"Oh."

"Do you want to go back?"

"No."

They went on, kicking at the ground until they recognized the outline of the merry-go-round in the funfair's center. It loomed out of the dark like a huge, sleeping crustacean, but became what it was, the closer they got. The animals in its grip were frozen in place, mid-crouch or mid-flight.

"I'll take that deer." It was green and pink; Magical ran ahead.

Emmett bleated before he could stop himself, "Not that one." He could not let her take that one. "I thought I might like to sit there."

Magical appeared not to notice the urgency. Likely, she had; she seemed to know how to walk around Emmett's grooves, rather than trying to reshape them.

She took the creature that hovered just ahead of the elk, a bull. Emmett would not have been able to see it, for it was painted the color of the night sky, but its rump was stuck all over with gilt stars and pasteboard gems that sparked when Magical struggled to mount it. She turned and faced him. Her legs, draped over the animal, were sturdy in their blue jeans; she hugged the beast with her thighs. On her feet was a pair of little black ankle boots. When cars passed on the highway, their headlamps cast a quick burst over her face, which was sharp and pert and full-lipped, full-lashed. Her hair had grown out a bit and curled around her ears. She was of this world, so much so that it enthralled him, frightened him. The other girls he'd admired, Renata, Delta, even this new girl whose name he did not yet know, were represented by nothing more than what his imagination could offer. Rex Henry told him stories about them. They had their relics, their trinkets. Longing was a beautiful thing; he'd longed for the girls, he'd longed for Rex Henry, and it was a vista that lasted into forever. But how long could you last, being kept at arm's length? It made him hate the girls, Rex Henry, too. Didn't they know how much it hurt?

And here was a girl called Magical John, who was looking at him, and who wanted him.

And, as the seconds passed, all the better to look at her—he wanted her, too.

She asked him before he could ask her: "Am I pretty?"

Emmett would have phrased it differently if he'd spoken first. But he was glad that Magical had. "Yes." He fingered the cowboy heart in his pocket. This was something he would not show to Rex Henry.

She dropped her head. Emmett feared that, through some mysterious turn of the heart's screws, he had made her cry. But when she righted herself, she was beaming, so pink he could see it through the dark. She was here, full, not some sacrosanct shadow.

He asked (another question he dared not put

to Rex Henry), "Am I—?"

Magical laughed. "Are you pretty? Yes, yes, you are. You are very pretty."

What Emmett did not know was that no one had ever called Magical John pretty. Emmett did not know her intimacies, her rashes, her disease, how the boys she knew pretended not to know her. Had love been a shadow for her, too?

She went on, "You have gorgeous green eyes and a good sharp nose. You have a good smile. You make me feel good when you look at me."

Emmett had never kissed anyone. He'd had to wait for someone to kiss him; Rex Henry had pushed him away the one time he'd tried. But now he had Magical John's hand in his, their arms reaching from the front end of the elk and the ass end of the bull. He pressed his lips to her fingers; he felt the edge of her ring in the corner of his mouth.

What did they do next? Emmett could not recall how he got from the elk to the bull, but there he was, pulled there, it seemed, by Magical John, who did not even have to touch him. They were joined, one feeding off the other through their clothes. Had their legs not been squeezed so tightly around the bull's middle, they might have collapsed, not to the ground, but into each other.

They might have been here for hours and they

would never have guessed. Around them, screeches and sputters, hisses and grunts, boars rutting in the grass, feral cats wrestling the only female into compliance. And Magical and Emmett had not been the only human tryst in the funfair's history. The floor of the merry-go-round was testament to that; whenever they came up for air, they read the graffiti, etched with jack-knives, scribbled with felt-tip pens.

> *Ricky & Darlene*
> *M and P were here*
> *Eric + Lynn-Lee forever*
> *S.P. & J.L. virgins no more 4.29.54*

Neither Emmett nor Magical said anything of it. Love between two people was commemorated in other ways, better ways. *Many waters cannot quench love, neither can the floods drown it.* Who said that? Didn't matter, it was better than *E.A. & M.J. virgins no more.*

An approaching headlamp doused them. The motor purred. Emmett leapt to his feet, covered Magical with his pea coat. No one came from the pickup, it just sat there at the fence, the eyes of the headlamps ogling at them like an all-knowing Peeping Tom.

Then a voice, deep from behind the eyes: "You missed supper."

Emmett would not say that he was sorry, only what happened. "Lost track of time."

"Well. You can eat on the way. I saved some for you here."

Emmett allowed the headlamps to pull him, for he was powerless. As an animal, he submitted to his bowels. As a man, he submitted to his beatitudes. When could he be Emmett Anhalt?

He turned. Magical had righted herself, stood, the pea coat draped from her shoulders. He was cold now and wanted her warmth. "You want us to give you a ride?" he called, damning what Rex Henry might have to say about it. "It's no trouble."

Magical slipped her arms into the sleeves. She was not looking at Emmett; for a moment, he was certain that, despite the cut of them, she was eyeing the headlamps. But that wasn't it either. Her gaze was trained over the hood, through the windshield. She buttoned the coat.

"It's not far," she said, "I can walk." And she came down the steps of the merry-go-round. And she stood on her toes, and she pressed a kiss into the corner of Emmett's lips.

"I'll be seeing you."

They had a year, for whatever that meant. He would see her again.

Emmett watched until a Skylark slowed at

the lip of the road and swallowed her, and he was alone.

In the Chevrolet, he unwrapped the tamale that Rex Henry had put aside for him. The truck's cab was scented with dried flowers; Emmett crunched rose petals with his fingers when he moved to close the door. Rex Henry drove at forty miles per hour, taking care to follow the speed limit to the T. He said, "She was going to be a nun."

Emmett's mind slipped over this. Magical, the ghost of her, hovered still in his mind's eye. In a minute, she faded, and her consecrated twin emerged. Her hair was dark and short, her eyes large, her dress modest. She carried her shoes on warm days. Emmett had seen her before he could see her. Perhaps it was because he now saw Magical in everything. It made him swell and tremble, and he reveled in the sensation.

"Her faculties are beyond reproach," Rex Henry intoned.

Emmett leaned his head against the window. Without knowing what he was saying, he murmured, *"She walks in beauty, like the night—"*

Rex Henry put in, *"I must walk right up to my last moment."* Saint Therese, the Little Flower.

"Where is she?"

"Who? Your lady-friend?"

"No. I know where she is."

"Do you?"

Emmett looked at him, bit into the tamale. "I do." Rex Henry did not approve of talking through mouthfuls.

"Well. She got into a car, she could be any-where."

"She's home. She's inside and she's warm. She's watching television." Emmett could not know this for sure, but he was right. At that moment, Magical had taken off her shoes and, still in Emmett's coat, curled into Granny Blanchefleur's davenport.

"Sounds nice. What's she watching?"

Emmett had never known the program sched-ule and Rex Henry did not have a TV. It made Emmett boil. He would not say *I don't know;* better to have the wrong answer than none at all. He reached. Finally, he said, *"Mystery Theater.* Yes, she's watching *Mystery Theater."* Another lucky guess, as it turned out, for there was Magical John, a pillow beneath her head and getting an eyeful of George Sanders.

All Emmett had in the meantime was the fracture in Rex Henry's surface. And he sat back, pleased.

"Well. I think one could find better things to do with one's time," Rex Henry allowed.

"Where is she?" Emmett wanted to stop talking about Magical John. Suddenly, it was not Rex Henry's place to speak of her, no matter how mild he was.

"She's resting," Rex Henry said, "not gone, as yet. But she's close."

He had not waited for Emmett. The rift had widened, the gates not barred, but closing. Emmett turned and gave Rex Henry his most beseeching look; he must have forgotten how to set his face, for Rex Henry seemed not to notice. *Let me stay with you. Let me stay with you.* "Where did you leave her?" Then, with a closing throat, "Won't someone see? If she's close?"

"She's close," Rex Henry said flatly, "She'll be just where I left her."

SPOOK SHOW

"Marilu. Marilu. Maria Luisa," her mother hissed, "don't pester the men. Go on and make yourself busy." And the little girl slumped into the kitchen to make coffee.

The law had been all over the cedar woods, up and down the highway, picking at the ground like vultures. They landed upon the drive-in first, only feet away from where the toe was found. The manager was no help, saying he saw nothing. "I only would know anything about it at all—because one of the kids started wailing. Then she says she saw someone. Two fellers. I had my barbecue boys look all around, but we couldn't find no one."

And now the law had come to call, two of that

great body this time, crammed into her mother's loveseat. The girl called Marilu dawdled over the coffee, putting Fig Newtons just so around the plate, eyeing the edge of the milk in the little calf-shaped jug to make sure it was level. She hovered in and out of the details, the whispers: they found a toe, they found hair, they found a finger bone. At one point, one half of the law mentioned something about the pieces being mismatched ("—may be looking at more than one—"); it made Marilu think of a film she'd seen, a Friday night spook show, a doctor assembling bits of what he could from different graves to make a new and whole man. *It's alive. IT'S ALIVE.*

Then the voices in the sitting room quieted, lower than whispers. Her mother said, "God." And they clammed right up when Marilu stepped in with the coffee tray.

"Thank you," the law said and sipped. "Appreciate all this, Mrs. Zamora."

"Now," one of them mumbled around a Fig Newton. He was looking at Marilu. "I know this must be awful to think on, dear, but it's very important. Just tell us what you can. Tell us what you saw."

This was the moment, and for this moment, Marilu would be a star. She sucked in her breath, like a singer preparing for the first note.

She opened her mouth.

PARADISE

LaRue Martin thought of Paradise. Her notion of it was not far away from what Emmett had imagined. A merry-go-round. Animals that clamored for the touch of her hand. Sugar in the air. She recalled having been there, just once, years ago. It was something that had kept with her always, and she could never track it, not then, and, to her disappointment, not now. She tried to place herself there, feel the chill in the air, taste the sugar. She was two. She wore a blue wool dress, she was unsteady on her feet. A cap on her head. In her mouth, she tasted apples.

Or was that now?

She was eighteen. She wore a blue wool dress,

she was unsteady on her feet. A cap on her head. In her mouth, she tasted bile.

But, here was the smell of sugar.

She was LaRue Martin and she was two years old, just as she was LaRue Martin and she was eighteen. She was going to ride the merry-go-round and she was going to the convent at Elam.

Paradise was youth, but she always knew that. Up to now, she'd never had time to consider why. It was the protection of it, yes, the embrace of an all-knowing guardian; she'd never been let out of her mother's sight. Her mother fed her, her father dressed her, they brought her on picnics to see the world through a rosy veneer. But that was only a bit of what made the connection between the two. All that time, however short it was, she'd been waiting for something. LaRue Martin was told, *When you're older, When you're bigger, Next year next year next year.* Christmas would always be coming up, the first day of summer vacation, her first C-rated movie, her driver's license, the Facts of Life and those awful pamphlets, the knowledge of good and evil. There was lots to look forward to.

That was youth. Was it Paradise?

In Paradise, you did the same thing every day, no past, no future, no change, no sorrows, no surprises, no growth.

LaRue blinked and kept her eyes open thereafter. She feared if she blinked again, that would be it. She shifted her lips, summoned her voice. *I don't want to go. I will not go. You can't make me go.* She managed to sputter, "NO."

THE PROMISED LAND

Emmett dropped to his knees. When he saw her, he wanted to die, too.

They came home, after a long drive, just around and around, as they'd done on Memorial Day. When Rex Henry parked, Emmett got his footing carefully, the way he would do in unfamiliar territory; even when his eyes sharpened and old shapes emerged, he was slow to trust them. He entered the house and did not disrobe.

Rex Henry moved to the back of the house, toward the bedroom. "Come on," he called, and Emmett, his Little Eminent, followed.

Rex Henry switched on the overhead light, so they saw the girl before the rest of the room. She filled the bed. She had short, dark hair that curled around her ears. She was stripped to the waist, allowed this much of her privacy, now in her last hours. Her breasts were in shreds. Emmett looked but did not find a knife or any kind of blade. Rex Henry's hands were large, and it was only here that Emmett noted how long the older man had always liked to keep the nails. They were dark, their undersides packed. They were furred, as the paws of a great and loathsome dog's. All the while, the girl's lips twitched; she was beyond agony, or the fullness of it had forced her to its libidinous opposite. Her legs were splayed. She did not try to hide herself beneath her skirt.

This was where Emmett dropped.

The bulb overhead was too bright.

"She was doing Renata's Walk," Rex Henry said, "of all things. We got a chance to talk a while. She told me she was headed for the convent at Elam. Bless her. How many young people do you find today who want nothing more than a life of contemplation? Her name is LaRue. That means, as the French say, *the street or the road*."

LaRue looked like Magical. Magical looked like LaRue.

Emmett watched the carpet until he saw the patterns in it.

When he came up for air, he tried to make

himself see the differences. LaRue was small, Magical solid and nearly as tall as Emmett. Magical would never allow herself to come to this place, to be in this bed, in this way. She loved her breasts, for one. She would have clawed Rex Henry blind, had he tried to remove them. Switching tactics, he looked at small LaRue Martin in disgust. He could just see it: alone on the road, picking up rides like the whey-faced little idiot that she was. Did it matter whether or not she was best beloved by the dregs of this world? Sainthood never stopped anyone from his or her own foolishness. Didn't she know what all they said about strangers and cars?

The girl opened her eyes, fixed them on Emmett. And for a long time afterward, they did not leave him.

Rex Henry had said of Magical, *She got into a car, she could be anywhere.*

"I can't." Emmett: steely or just impotent? He put a fingertip to LaRue's smallest toe and she flinched. Then she convulsed; the bedframe screeched. Here was a Sister of Adoration in its throes. He backed away until he felt the bureau against his shoulder blades. "I told you before. I can't." He wondered if she knew the day, the hour, and was simply following her course to its end.

Rex Henry settled into the armchair in the corner of the room, where he always set out his clothes for the next day. He lit a cigarette and made a stony audience to the girl in the bed, whom he had ravished, who had submitted to his ravishing before she knew what was happening. She'd been telling him of the convent at Elam, at the same time as she'd been imagining her union with her Beloved, her white gown. All the while, it was dark, the car made turns, it took her a moment to realize that this was not the way. His thumb in her throat. He hadn't needed a tool, he never really had.

"Well, as it turns out," he sighed, "you don't need to do a thing. Lucky you missed supper, I suppose. Oh, now, don't do that—" He rose to where Emmett had curled himself and pulled the boy's hand from between his teeth. The meat of Emmett's hand was rough with scar tissue. Rex Henry moved to undo the buttons of the boy's plaid shirt; he did not so much calm as go absolutely rigid. Rex Henry's voice cracked. "Let me."

Emmett softened, only a bit. "I don't want to," he muttered.

"You don't have to."

Meanwhile, LaRue Martin stilled and her eyes froze on the space between Emmett's collar and his throat. Where did she go after? Emmett hoped, for his sake and for hers, that this was it, that there was nowhere else to go.

Rex Henry paused, Emmett's shirt in his hands. He sighed, shuddering, ecstatic. "You don't have to."

Emmett could not sleep and he could not read and if he ate, the food would not stay down. He had nothing else to do but watch Rex Henry render the girl with a butcher's precision. Some pieces he kept, a tooth, a toe. The rest he buried by the apple trees, in pits so shallow, Emmett thought of the fingers poking through the soil with the spring green. He could not resist the tooth; no matter what happened, he would never stop collecting. He cupped it and kissed it. He peered through the window to watch Rex Henry, heaving up and down, the shovel's spray flying into the early dawn. It was a much less fastidious procedure than in days passed.

He asked the older man why. Rex Henry stood in the shower and filled the house with steam and Head and Shoulders. Emmett sat in the hallway and moved to the kitchen when he heard the water shut off. He made tea and, because his appetite was creeping back, cracked and whipped and scrambled eggs for the two of them. The morning was deep, red, still dark.

Rex Henry, robed, took his place at the table and remarked, "Red sky at night, sailors' delight. Red sky at morning, sailors take warning."

Emmett added milk to his tea. The mug he drank from had a pattern of dogs running painted on it. He couldn't tell if it was a parade of dogs or just the one, galloping, galloping, galloping. "Well?"

"Hm?"

"What's the deal?" Emmett jerked his head to the window. "Out there?" Rex Henry only left as much as he wanted.

And Rex Henry took his time to answer, and not for any lack of one. He started on the eggs, adding salt or pepper, dabbing the hot sauce just so, stirring a fingertip's worth of brown sugar into his tea. He ate slowly, his tongue working to savor each bite. Every so often, he would drop his fork and watch the sky go from red to pink, the branches shuddering. Even the smallest things, the grains of salt on the tabletop, droplets of tea from when he lifted the bag from the cup, the wax paper that enveloped the butter. Emmett found himself trying to do the same and, to Rex Henry's credit, his mind quieted.

At last, Rex Henry announced that it was time for the two of them to make amends with the world.

Emmett's stomach churned, but he listened.

"We haven't done wrong, I want you to understand that."

228

Emmett nodded.

"But we need to think about their people. They live day to day. They're angry now, and they think that will last into forever. But one day, believe it or not, this will all make sense to them, just as much as it does to you and me. The big picture. Think of Pilate."

He told Emmett not long ago of the prefect of Judea, who was exiled, for washing his hands or not washing his hands. He went to France, to Switzerland, to Ponza in Italy. He converted, he drowned himself, the Emperor Caligula had him beheaded. This was not in the scriptures, but then the scriptures themselves seemed more and more a jumble to him as it went on. The story seemed to change every time.

Rex Henry said, "We'll take a few days. Just the two of us. We'll take these days to enjoy ourselves. How's that sound?"

MOST PRECIOUS BLOOD

They rode around, from Andermatt to El Velo, into Himmel Creek, where, wouldn't you know it, the ice cream shop was open, even though it was January; Rex Henry had hot chocolate, Emmett had a Snow White, its vanilla twin. They went hiking on Elam's rocky trails at sunrise, watched the bats return to their roosts in a bridge's underside. "These ones ought to have migrated back in the fall," Rex Henry noted as a squealing black cloud drew closer. "But some stick around." They went to Dear Liza's Café, where they sat and listened to Sun Ra and His Arkestra on the jukebox. They sat on the steps outside the general store and drank bottles of Big Red. This was a bright and friendly time, it was almost too much. Everyone greeted them with smiles, nods, folks called from across streets, "Hey, how're yew today? Y'all been keeping warm?"

It was cold and Emmett, for once, felt the edge of it. He missed his pea coat and wrapped himself in layers of sweaters and flannel. He was glad that Magical had it, though. Most mornings were frost-laden and she had to walk to school. At two-thirty, when Phillip D. Andermatt High let out, he would watch for her in the exiting stream. There she was, every time, bundled into his coat, sometimes with a fluffy scarf added or a lavender beret. It took real restraint to keep from calling to her.

What is the difference between a thing that is quiet and a thing that is ordinary?

Rex Henry downed the last of his pop and stood. "I'm going to the gents'. You want to wait out here?"

Magical had already vanished into the road, and Emmett was sure that she was safe in her grandmother's house. No point in freezing. He rose, followed the older man into the general store.

The Christmas décor still adorned the counter, one of the windows; while the management had seen fit to take down the Santa Clauses and the red-and-green bits, they had left the silver tinsel and the colored lights, which worked together to reflect pink and green and gold from every corner. Emmett sat at the counter, swiveled on it, studied the doodads and posters on the walls. Sunday night was a spaghetti dinner at the Sweet Home Baptist Church. The Andermatt County Ladies' Club. Eagle Scouts. The Knights of Columbus were meeting in the Masonic Lodge. Notices for the musical at the high school, *The Mikado*. An old poster for *Saint Joan*; he remembered something funny that he'd wanted to tell Magical, that Joan of Arc's last words were, "Jesus, Jesus, Jesus," at which point he would say, "She was on fire, after all."

And there, where he should have seen it first, was Rex Henry's face. His, too. A crude sketch, inky portraits side by side, no names, but a caption in blocky print: *HAVE YOU SEEN THESE MEN?* Emmett couldn't read more. Though the drawings were no better than cartoons (Rex Henry's nose too fat, Emmett's eyes so downturned they called to mind those of a Bassett hound), it didn't take long to see who was who.

Emmett told Rex Henry about it in the Chevrolet.

Rex Henry nodded. "Noted the color of the car and everything." The radio played, the local station, which was usually gospel or rousing, folksy stuff, covers by county people. It was Hillgrass Blue Billy's Flower Hour. Here was the next number, a little ginger-haired gal with a great big voice, please welcome Andermatt's own Emily Kitchen. Rex Henry turned it up. "I'll be. Look who it is."

Emily sang, *"She's only a bird in a gilded cage…"*

Her voice was not what Emmett had expected of her, so puny, so crippled. It was full-bodied with a purring undercurrent, coming from her throat like a grown woman's. He mentioned this to Rex Henry, who said, "Isn't that always true of great singers? Edith Piaf's four-foot-ten. Judy Garland, five feet, if she's lucky. We might never know they were there, otherwise."

"She's younger than me." Emmett didn't know his age and he didn't know Emily Kitchen's either, but the girl did not strike him as his senior, even by a minute.

"Well. That's the way of great singers, too. Farinelli was fifteen when he made his debut." Rex Henry thought. "They'd gelded him, so he would have the voice he'd have. Nonetheless."

It seemed to Emmett that love, reverence, immortality came to you based not so much on what you had as much as what you didn't. Or what you didn't do.

Emmett, to his knowledge, had everything, ears and eyes that worked, his manhood, his hair and all his teeth. He was tall and never crippled. He ate anything, did not restrict himself of any pleasures, great or small. He'd cursed in Magical's

234

company and felt the tiny release that came with shouting "RATFUCK" at cars that did not stop to pick them up. It added up to an anger so small he nearly quashed it but, like a fly that kept buzzing and buzzing in his brain, the more he swatted, the more it swarmed.

Rex Henry retraced their route well into the afternoon. Emily Kitchen had more than the regular time allotted on Hillgrass Blue Billy's, and neither he nor Emmett wanted to miss it. She covered a few more songs, "They Can't Take That Away from Me," "We'll Meet Again," "Like Someone in Love," "La Vie en Rose." Jazz standards, not the Flower Hour's usual thing. Hillgrass Blue Billy was out of luck when it came to finding anyone local with real talent. It was a good day if he aired someone's grandmother singing "Danny Boy." Emily Kitchen would go far, and Hillgrass Blue Billy would say he knew her when. For now, her audience, her first fans, sat in a Chevrolet pickup the color of a raw heart and basked. Her voice settled the two of them like wine.

"Well, we'd love to keep her for as long as we can, but we've only time for one more number." Hillgrass Blue Billy did sound sorry to see her go. "Now, what're you going to sing for us?"

One note, and Emily's voice, *I fall in love too easily…*

Rex Henry parked in the post office lot and they did not move until the last of the girl's warmth and wine moved through the airwaves. He was about to pull out when Emmett flapped his hand. "Wait. Wait, there's more."

And there was. As it turned out, Hillgrass Blue Billy was giving over the day's Flower Hour and more to a tribute concert, performed by the Phillip D. Andermatt High School choir. "Direct from the Phillip D. Andermatt Auditorium. In loving memory of three of our own dear singers, our own beloved students, Renata Ansky, Delta Lynn Bohannon, LaRue Therese Martin." Renata, the freshman. Delta, the graduate. LaRue, the senior. Renata had liked to read, Delta had liked to cook, LaRue had liked to sew. They all had liked to sing. "And so," Hillgrass Blue Billy announced, "we'll sing to them."

And the choir sang, unaccompanied, filling the car, the air, a polyphony of voices, layer upon layer to build a single, glorious sound. They sang "Nearer, My God, to Thee." Emmett wondered if the program was live, for, shortly after the last note had faded, there remained a funny little echo outside, not far away, coming from the school.

Rex Henry and Emmett sat. They were quiet. They watched the sky change and the leaves skitter across the parking lot.

Finally, Rex Henry said, "It's getting on for five o'clock."

Emmett knew what was coming. He nodded.

"I'd like to get some stamps before they close up." Rex Henry looked to the post office, whose lights were still bright. Through the window, you could see the edge of the desk, the grid of post boxes along the walls. "They've got those wildlife conservation ones out. If we don't get them now, we never will."

Emmett thought about stamps. His mother had collected them, she had an album of them that she kept out of Emmett's reach. "That's precious cargo," she'd say, "One day, I'll sell those and you won't believe how much I'll bring in. People buy them for up to thousands of dollars." They were pretty and his mother organized them by their respective collections. The Presidents, the seasons, holidays, state flowers, state parks, state pies.

He did not want to think about what would follow. But he would not make a move to stop it. He switched the station to one from Austin, the one that they played most often, in the car, at home.

And here was Chet Baker. *I fall in love too easily…*

Emmett reached for Rex Henry's hand, and he thought of Magical. She was home, walking her yard, wrapped in his coat. This could be enough. He had Rex Henry. This could be enough.

"I love this song," Emmett murmured.

Rex Henry squeezed. "Me, too."

Fingers laced, they waited until the last of Chet Baker had faded into the airwaves.

Emmett swallowed a few times, then sighed. "All right," he said. "I'm ready."

The poster was the first thing they saw, behind the clerk's grill. It was nearly buried beneath the layers of leftover Christmas doodads, paper snowflakes and golden tinsel, but it set them off as prettily as a frame. All the mess inside Emmett was very quickly turning into something else. Perhaps it was all the gilt and glitter around the place, but even now, whatever came next, he felt something like excitement. His hands twitched in his pockets, and it was all he could do to keep from dancing.

Rex Henry went to the desk. The clerk busied himself with the register and looked at him, looked at him again, looked at him again. The clerk had had to look at the poster many times since they'd put it up, and he'd tried to think of where he had seen that face before, a pop in the crowd before it vanished into someone else. Like an angel or a demon, you could never catch a thing like that. And now, this creature presented himself, seemingly with no other purpose than for Ivo Ansky to tell
238

the world that he was real.

From beyond the grave, the Blessed Renata glowed and was gone.

Rex Henry said, "One book of stamps, please."

Emmett, behind him, rocked on his heels.

Ivo Ansky scattered papers as he grappled for the phone, scattering the floor with preserved American wildlife.

DUST AND LIGHT

The law went to their house and found toes and teeth in the bureau. They handled the bedsheet that had soaked up the last of LaRue Martin like a holy shroud. In the yard, they found the girl herself. It was difficult to piece her together, for she shared a grave with a beloved family dog.

The law saw the animal's marker and declared it a miracle. "Thirty years old. That's got to be the oldest pooch in the world."

At the roadside, Magical John buttoned her pea coat. She watched and would not weep.

VESPERS

It was all so quick, Emmett hadn't time to grasp it all.

His mother had come to see him, once he and Rex Henry were situated in the Andermatt County jail. She hadn't anything to say, she just wanted to get a good look at him. Did she see what her only boy had made of himself? He couldn't tell. She stared and she breathed. She wore a brown dress with a straight skirt and a pair of Aunt Jewel's coral earrings shaped like rosebuds. She had a note for him from Aunt Jennie. It read, *Pray for me. It will mean more from you than anyone.*

He tried to write Aunt Jennie a letter for his mother to send back. He would start by saying,

You're. And he would cross out whatever came next. *You're a witch. You're forgiven. You're unclean.* He tried to quote, as Rex Henry did. *All shall be well, and all shall be well, and all manner of thing shall be well.* He thought he ought to feel like a saint writing that, but the more he looked at it, the more it struck him as the kind of phrase you'd needlepoint. In the end, he scrawled in block letters, *Will do.*

He learned that he was eighteen. It seemed that this was the source of great commotion, for no one knew how to address him. Was he a boy or a man? What was the state going to do with him? Now that his birthday had passed (and when had that happened? It was March now), it was all made clear, tensions eased, and they let him stay where he was. If he were still a boy, Emmett would have been crammed in with other boys, full of noise and blood and lust, and he would rather have died than to have lived that.

Rex Henry was in the next cell. Emmett could not see him, but they could touch, snaking one hand through the bars to link with the other, and they would fall asleep this way.

There was no mob, no vengeful howling for blood. Not even the parents of those blessed girls made a threat, at least not that they had heard, and despite being locked in, life went on, news still carried. There was no mob, but there were people. They left letters at first, sympathetic yet sanctimonious. *I can't begin to understand why you did what you did. A normal person couldn't understand. I will say this: you are a creature of God. You are blessed, too. Whatever happens, it is in His will. You know that, I think, as well as I do.* Then came offerings—charity provisions, really, from the Ladies' Club or the Freemasons. Emmett and Rex Henry received books, lots of poetry, a complete Shakespeare, a King James Bible. Then, from those who sought to put an end to the chair altogether, came flowers, the first apple blossoms from the orchards. These were the people who did not cast stones, the ones for whom all were innocent, despite the evidence. They said of Emmett and Rex Henry, *Judge not, that ye be not judged.* They wrote to them, *We have faith in you. The system is quick to find a scapegoat. We won't let you fall thru the crack.*

The talk from the outside went back and forth:

They did it.

We don't know if they did it.

They ought to get the chair.

All life is precious.

A lot of declarations, but no one did anything, save for the books and the flowers.

Emmett had tried, for a while, to make a home for himself here. He'd undressed, as he'd always done, but the floors were cold and, as though a light in him had been switched off, he could see the guards see him. So he enveloped himself in blankets or disrobed only during the small hours, when he nor Rex Henry could sleep.

VISITATION

Renata and Delta and LaRue gathered at their feet. In life, they had all been small, and now they looked down at Rex Henry and Emmett. They glowed. They wore gowns of tulle and velvet— LaRue had made them for all three girls. They crowded together and looked as though they might serenade the two men; they'd sung in life, after all.

Instead, they stuck out their tongues and blew.

Rex Henry had no visitors, though Emmett had two. His mother had come, and then Magical John.

It was April and hot again. Still, she wore his

coat and under that, a pair of pink shorts and a white t-shirt.

"Aren't you roasting in that?" Emmett's shirt stuck to him.

Magical shook her head. She hadn't yet said so much as Hello. She stared, as the rest of them did from the outside.

Then, from Emmett, sudden and snappish, "Take that off."

From his cell, Rex Henry called, "Watch your tone, there."

Magical sat back, crossed her legs. When she was sure Rex Henry had buried himself once again in his book, she pulled a face, eyes crossed, tongue wagging. It reminded Emmett of the raspberries Renata and Delta and LaRue had given him and Rex Henry the night before; he could still feel the spittle on his cheeks. Who knew saints made such faces?

"Don't do that," he hissed, though it was also a comfort to see Magical and her old irreverence.

Like that, she stopped. She turned back to him. "I wish I had something to bring you. Like a crossword, or something." She peered behind him into the cell, which was crammed with books, papered with letters, gifts from do-gooders.

"I have plenty."

"What about snacks? Do they let people bring you food?"

"They're afraid you'll hide something in it, like a knife."

"Oh. That's right."

"Anyway, we're fed all right. Dear Liza's brings us breakfast and supper."

Magical nodded. "That's good of them."

"It's food. We eat it."

"You sure there's nothing I can bring—"

Emmett seethed. He snarled and slapped his palm against his thigh. "Could you just stop saying that? Please?"

And he got something out of her again, her face sharpening and her eyes no longer dewy, but sparking around the edges. Before she could go soft again, she barked, "Well, shit. I'm ever so sorry. If I'd known you were going to get like that, I wouldn't've come."

This was better. Emmett sighed, reached for her hand. "I just don't want anymore stuff, is all."

Magical allowed a tiny smile. "Not even from me?"

Emmett listened for Rex Henry. For the last fifteen minutes or so, the neighboring cell had been full of low, rhythmic breaths. And they hadn't

251

stopped; Emmett could never tell if the older man was sleeping or deep in contemplation. It was all the more ominous, now that Emmett could not see him.

Magical took the cue and peeked. "He's asleep."

"You sure?"

"He's in bed. He's got the pillow over his ear."

Emmett drew closer. So did Magical, who said again, "So. No presents, even from me?"

Emmett brought one of her fingers to his mouth. He tasted her salt. "Especially not from you."

"Can I still come?"

"Yes. Oh, yes." Emmett rose as she did. Before she was brought away, he called, "Will you come tomorrow?"

She looked back, not far enough away to be heard: "And every day after."

He shouted, before the doors locked once more, "And stop wearing that coat. You'll roast."

Renata and Delta and LaRue came again in their gowns of velvet and tulle. They did not sing, nor did they make faces. They stood and they whispered and they giggled, as girls do. It was all so sweet that for much of the night, Emmett could ignore the hard fact that the girls were laughing at him. Rex Henry, too, and this was a shock. No one laughed at Rex Henry.

They told them that they smelled. Emmett sniffed his underarms; he'd been let to shower that morning, before meeting with his attorney.

Rex Henry intoned from the next cell, "Keep strong. You're made of better stuff than that. And they know it. They wouldn't have come, other-wise."

Still, Emmett sniffed and sniffed in every crevice. He ought not to care about such things, but it was suddenly a great terror, having to sit here in his own stink and be chastised for the foulness of it.

He tried, just once, to make it right. He looked to Delta, the tallest of them, the oldest. She would be forever twenty, pretty. Her madness was a testament to her divinity. In time, her scribbles on the *Readers' Digest* would become collectors' items. He knelt and pleaded, "I only got one. Tell them, go on. You were the only one."

Delta Bohannon stood away from the others. In that moment, Emmett thought he had her alone.

Rex Henry called to him from the next cell, "I wouldn't do that, if I were you."

And she rushed at Emmett, banging at the bars, howling, drooling, shrieking, laughing, her eyes red and her nails long, heaving as he ducked into his cot. He did not remove the pillow from his ear until sunup.

Emmett had been told to keep quiet. Rex Henry had said it would be for the good of all they had done. "They'll come to rest, and so will we. Just give them what they want."

The girls would enter Paradise. And so would they.

All Emmett had to do was to follow Rex Henry.

They were let to put on free-wear clothes on this day. The Ladies' Club had collaborated with the Freemasons and wrangled up a suit for Rex Henry, a collared shirt and corduroys for Emmett. They had to look their best, for everyone would see them, everyone would remember them, down to the shine of their shoes.

The last time Andermatt County had anyone put to death was 1900: In the spring of that year, a goat farmer by the name of Pooky Essen stabbed a young shepherdess, ten-year-old Ivy Rauschenberg, fourteen times with an awl. His motive was unclear. The people hissed and spat at the sight of him. A woman shouted again and again from a bar-

barous crowd, "I WANT THAT MAN DEAD."
His hanging was public, medieval in its festivity:
there were sausage and lemonade stands, shills for
bets on how long Essen would dangle, picnics on
the Andermatt green, folks with kids, folks with
dogs. No one heard his last words, for the volume
of the audience.

Essen was pilloried, not pedestaled.

Emmett had read about him in a volume of
court minutes and had brought his name up when
he could.

The guardsman asked, "Pooky who?"

His attorney asked, "Who's that, now?"

Mrs. Nimitz from the Ladies' Club said,
"Sounds like something from the funny papers."

Magical John said, "Never heard of him."

It was almost better, Emmett thought, to
have had to run that gauntlet in those last minutes
than to be remembered forever. When you were
remembered forever, people studied you. People
pulled you apart.

But wasn't that the best thing about being
remembered? People studying you and pulling you
apart? When had Emmett ever been the subject of
real scrutiny? It was too seductive to deny.

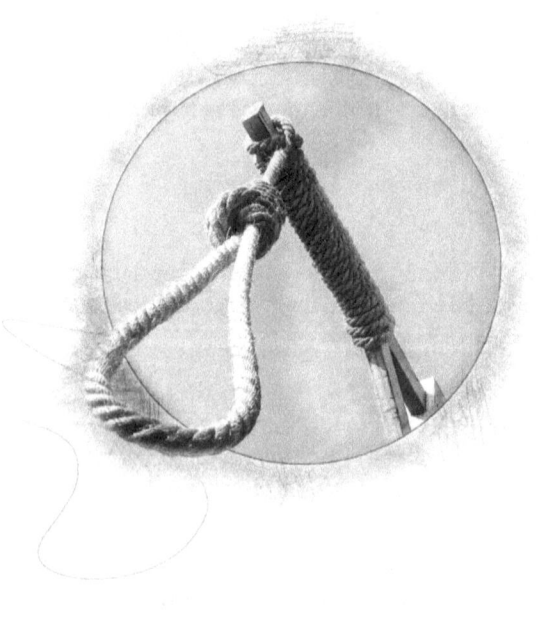

VERDICT

Today, the crowd that awaited Rex Henry and Emmett was quiet, well-behaved. They parted for the two men as they moved, shackled, from the Black Maria to the courthouse. There were no concessions, no gambling. No one said a word. Perhaps it was because people knew them. But Andermatt County was small, and it could only have been smaller in 1900. Perhaps it was because people liked them. But Pooky Essen had been married with seven children; someone had liked him, too.

What is the difference between a thing that is quiet and a thing that is ordinary?

Someone touched Emmett. Another blessed him from far away. No one seemed to grant Rex

Henry these benedictions; perhaps it was because Emmett was young. Like an acquaintance you pretend not to see, the people allowed Rex Henry to pass, looking through him, seeing Emmett first.

Emmett allowed himself to smile, just a bit, just enough to thank his well-wishers. He thought little of it until Rex Henry fell behind to lean into the spiral of his ear. He hissed, "Wipe that grin off your face, pretty boy."

It was as though Rex Henry had unzipped himself, just for a moment, all lewdness and stink. It was a Rex Henry that Emmett had never heard. There was grime in his voice.

For the Lord thy God is a jealous God among you.

Therefore, Emmett was left to do nothing but to follow him and keep quiet. The crowd and the glory faded around him and there was nothing left but the two of them. He did not register the flashbulbs or the change from outdoors to in. All the while, he schemed ways to bring himself back into Rex Henry's good graces, and each one lifted and deflated. What was the point? Rex Henry had to come in his own time. Such as it was, it would forever be.

Emmett sat beside Rex Henry and looked at him. *Come back to me. When will you come back to me? Come back to me.*

Rex Henry kept straight ahead. For all he cared at this hour, he was alone and too big for anyone.

The judge read the verdict. "For the murder of Renata Ansky, I sentence you to be electrocuted until you are dead. For the murder of Delta Lynn Bohannon, I sentence you to be electrocuted until you are dead. For the murder of LaRue Therese Martin, I sentence you to be electrocuted until you are dead."

There. Like that.

In the gods, Renata and Delta and LaRue laughed because they could not speak. Anyone else who had seen them would never have believed that, in life, they really were very nice girls. Expiration had made hags of them.

Rex Henry looked ahead.

Emmett looked inward, where the girls wanted him to go. He stood and vomited. It was all anyone in Andermatt County could talk about for days.

He's afraid for his soul.

He's sorry.

He couldn't have said which he was.

RESURRECTION

Magical John had not gone to the court-house. She had not gone to school. She told her grandmother that she had a horrible attack of something-or-other and could not bear the walk to school. She slept late and ate sparingly. Granny Blanchefleur, ever-wary of school-borne epidemics, let Magical stay at home for as long as the trial had gone on.

Magical itched until she bled. She'd slept in the pea coat, which proved to be an attraction to the fleas brought in by the cat. She wept and so did her markings.

She would go mad. The coat was all she had of him. She could not have said whether to damn or coddle herself for this foolishness. She lay in her bed, watched the patterns in the ceiling dance and shift. Her record player never stilled. It filled the house with the soppy crooners her grandmother had thought she'd like. They'd sat dusty for months under her bed. Now Granny Blanchefleur was threatening to burn them.

"There's plenty of room in the incinerator," she called, paper bags in hand. "And if there isn't, I'll make room."

Take my hand, I'm a stranger in Paradise…

Magical waited until the last of Bing Crosby wavered, softened, and stopped. She went to her little bathroom, papered with blue hydrangeas, and sat. Urination was less painful now, but it came in frequent dribblings, urgent as they seemed. She felt like a broken percolator. Emptied, she stomped back to her bedroom and gathered the crooners' records by the armload.

"Well." In the yard, Granny Blanchefleur fanned herself with a magazine. She paused to poke through the stack in Magical's arms. "Leave me the Nat King Cole. I always liked him." Then, she stood back, eyed her granddaughter up and down. "You must be sick. Your face is all swole."

A blaze brewed in the incinerator's gut. Remnants of newspaper, crumbling leaves, bones of the things the cat brought home. Magical held her free hand toward the flames, though it must have been eighty degrees out.

Granny spoke again. "Your stomach's not upset?"

"What's that?"

Granny sucked her teeth. She hated to repeat herself. "I say, your stomach's not upset?"

"No."

"Well." Granny Blanchefleur nodded. She swallowed and eased into the kitchen chair she'd brought out, folded the magazine's pages into pleats, tore them into strips. Finally, she sighed, "Well. Neither did I. Carried three babes and I always kept my food down."

Granny Blanchefleur knew the tides of the moon and its relation to people. She knew when her granddaughter waxed and when she waned. Magical had not bled since Christmas. She didn't know who she was fooling.

Since Christmas, she had been content to leave it to her own will. Here came the old clichés: *You don't pick who you love, It happens when you least expect it, Love happens in cottages as well as in courts.* And Magical sifted through each of them, and she came to a decision: she was not to blame, and the boy was not to blame, and the devil in her was not to blame. It was not retribution, but nature, going along as it did, taking its course. Magical felt with her organs and nerves. Her soul would die with its vessel; she'd made peace with that idea long ago. She was fragile enough to expire, strong enough to carry another life. Magical John would take credit for that, any day.

She would bring her belly to Emmett and he would touch it.

Granny Blanchefleur wadded the magazine strips into a ball. "You know what? You want to leave me the Rudy Vallee, too? The others, do what you want." She shot the paper ball into the flames. "Just keep an eye on it. Don't want to start a brushfire."

Bing Crosby and all the rest leaked into the refuse, the papers, the leaves and the bones. Magical knelt at Granny's chair. She let her head sink lower and lower until she was pillowed by her grandmother's lap where Granny's hand pulled at the growing ply of her hair.

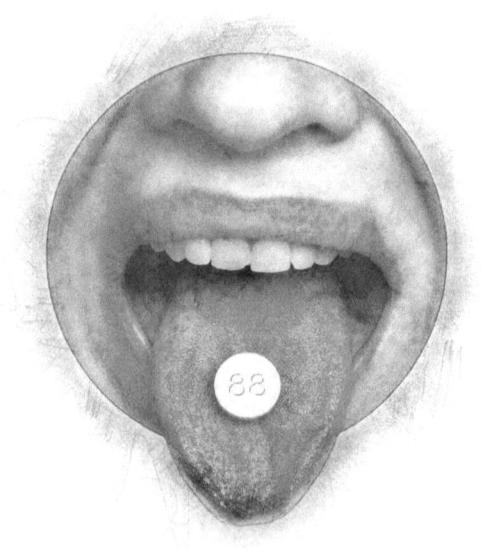

CURTAIN CALL

Emmett asked Rex Henry through the wall, "Were you ever married?"

A shuffling and scraping, the sounds of a toothbrush. "Once."

"What was it like?"

"It lasted for as long as it was meant to."

"But what was it like?"

"It was fair."

Fair meant a lot of things. Emmett's marks at school had, for the most part, been Fair. A blue sky could be called fair. A beautiful woman in a romance. Somehow, Emmett likened Rex Henry's use of the word to his marks: decent enough, but

267

nothing to give three cheers about.

Emmett tried again. He pressed his cheek against the stucco. "What was her name?"

A creak from the cot, the powdery notes of pages turning. "What was who?"

"Your wife." It was an odd thing to imagine Rex Henry having. Rex Henry belonged to no one, not even Emmett.

"Well." Rex Henry paused to dog-ear his place. "I believe it was Lena. No—" he coughed, "—no, perhaps it was Lorna. It was some years ago."

There was nowhere else for Rex Henry to go. Emmett could ask him anything now. He was almost afraid to, for the fear that the older man might grow smaller and smaller the more Emmett knew.

But he pressed on. "How old were you when you married?"

"Seventeen."

"For how long were you married?"

"For as long as I saw fit."

"But for how long?"

"Under ten years."

"Why aren't you married now? Is she dead?"

"No."

"Are you divorced?" Emmett knew that his Aunt Jewel was divorced, a marriage so quick it might as well have never happened. Six months was under ten years, too.

"No." And Rex Henry very quickly explained the concept of annulment.

"Do you hear from her still?"

"I got a letter from her about twenty years ago. A Christmas card, really."

"Do you have it?"

"Not on me, no."

"Is it still in your house?" In his mind, Emmett began the orchestrations of uncovering it, getting someone from the outside to dig through the bowels of the bedroom, the closets—

"I believe I threw it away."

"Why?"

"More clutter than needed."

Emmett's mother, now that he thought of it, never threw anything away. She kept every birthday card, Christmas card, sympathy card and so on in shoeboxes, which she shelved along with her winter clothes at the back of her closet. Emmett had liked to sort through them quite a lot. Once, ages ago, he came across one addressed to him.

Inside, under *Should auld acquaintance be forgot in 1950*, was written in smeary pencil, *Here's hoping we meet one day, if not this year, then in the near future. Hello to your mother for me. Best, Ray McKnight.* His mother deliberated for a minute after he showed it to her. In the end, she'd let honesty win. Ray McKnight was his father. Of course, Emmett had questions and his mother supplied answers: Ray McKnight had rented a room from her years ago, the one Aunt Jewel now slept in. He did handiwork, a little of this, a little of that. He left when his lease was up and they'd written, on and off. At the time the card was sent, Ray McKnight had lived in New Mexico, in a place called San Ildefonso Pueblo. He'd gone out there to become a potter and return to his roots, Emmett's mother had said of him, and she'd huffed slightly. "He said his great-great-grandmother was an Indian princess. Him and everyone else's great-great-grandmother." But she'd grown quiet for a moment, then said, "You want to write him? I saved the envelope. He put an address on it." Emmett had shaken his head. From what his mother had given him, he could just about piece together the kind of man Ray McKnight was. At the time, Ray McKnight had seemed like a drip.

And it was funny. It wasn't so difficult to imagine Rex Henry renting Aunt Jewel's old room, doing a little of this, a little of that, going off to the desert to slap clay when he was through. It was almost comical, like the end of *The Wizard of Oz*. All along, fat little Professor Marvel was the voice behind that smoldering head. *Pay no attention to that man behind the curtain!* He'd bellowed.

But here was the thing: Rex Henry could answer you or not. It was when he answered that was key. It built Emmett up for the new campaign. It reminded him of his place on the pedestal. And just as easily, Rex Henry could knock him from his place.

He bet Ray McKnight couldn't do that.

For now, Rex Henry had gone silent. It took longer than Emmett wanted to admit that he had been talking to the wall. He pressed his ear against the stucco, strained his eyes through the bars and tried to angle his head just so. But he heard nothing and he saw nothing. Time passed. Supper came: city chicken, rice, butter beans, a peanut butter cookie. Rex Henry had to eat. Emmett listened as he took his tray; he would never know if the older man were there, otherwise.

Emmett started on the rice. He waved for the guard who'd served them. "What's that for?" He pointed to an intersection in the tray, the point at which the corners of the four compartments met. On it was a tablet, sky blue, about the size of Emmett's littlest fingernail.

The guard craned his head and squinted. "Blue

88, it looks like to me."

"What's it for?"

"It makes you sleep."

"I sleep fine." Though his dreams pulsed the night through, the girls seemed to have surrendered. Emmett had not seen Renata and Delta and LaRue since the sentencing.

The guard coughed. "Then it'll make you calm." He didn't quite look at Emmett, not into his face. He studied pieces of the young man, his hands, the bridge of his nose, his collarbone.

Rex Henry had rejected every appeal, which meant Emmett had, too. In another month, the pair of them would be made ready for the four-hour drive to Huntsville. From there, they would depart this world together. Emmett could not see where there was to go without the older man.

"I'm fine." Emmett said this and it was true. The more he thought of it, the less expiration frightened him. He realized that he'd stopped thinking of Paradise, and when he did, it was with great reluctance. All that cajeta, the ever-winding merry-go-round. It grated at him, like a song that never ended. He would rather have it over and done with. But he didn't tell Rex Henry that.

"Regardless. I'm to watch you take it, once you've finished supper." The guard backed into the folding chair and positioned himself in between the cells. He looked to Emmett. "If nothing else, it makes you loopy. I was in Belgium during the war. In a clinic for a month. They shelled it out like candy. I felt like I was made out of water, all that time."

It sounded very like a dream Emmett had had, in one of his last nights at Rex Henry's. He'd been floating along a stream, coursing toward a rock. All the while, he felt sure that he would loop around it, like a blade of grass. But he surged ahead, the rock face coming at him, an imminent collision—and he woke, stiff and wet and cold.

Emmett gnawed at what he could of the city chicken (breaded pork, wasn't it?). He saved the glass of milk for last, half for the cookie, the other half to wash down the tablet. In the corridor, the guard nodded to the adjacent cell. He appraised Rex Henry, saying, "It'll take the edge off. I'd offer you some Old Crow to go with that, if I could."

Emmett heard Rex Henry, a bit muffled. "I'm not a drinking man."

The guard shifted in his chair. "Fair enough." He turned to Emmett. "Get that down, son."

Emmett didn't want to feel like water. His body aped the motions of obedience, putting the tablet in the square center of his tongue, downing the last of the milk. All the while, his mouth rebelled; his tongue, manipulative, worked until the tablet was tucked safely beneath it. He unhinged his jaw for the guard, who gave him a thumb's up. "There's a good boy."

The overhead lights never dimmed, but there were a few unsupervised hours along the hall. Emmett used this time wisely. Before bed, he urinated and flushed the tablet with his refuse.

LUST OF EYES

Marilu was in hot water. She'd carved graffiti into Delta Bohannon's Fairlane while she was meant to be collecting entry fees for the drive-in's manager. The manager gave her a little cut now and then from a Saturday's earnings. But lately, he'd determined that, because of her age, Marilu ought to be happy with fifty cents, then forty, then thirty-five. It was always a handful of loose change, never anything as concrete as two quarters. Did he think they didn't teach simple money counting in the second grade? When she opened her mouth to argue, the manager spat, "What're you saving for? College?" Then, in his ugliest tone, he made his threat, "I got a phone book. It won't take too much out of my day to call your mama up and tell her what you've really been up to."

Mrs. Zamora thought that her daughter was going to the Fairlane to contemplate her soul with the other devotees. She'd boasted of Marilu's new-found piety at Ladies' Club meetings. She'd have her little girl's neck if she found out.

Still, it wasn't enough. And so, after she'd told the manager she was off to the woods for a pee break, she'd ducked behind the Fairlane, stray nail in hand. The devotees were too ruminative to hear the screep-screep outside the car. She stepped back to admire. There it was, a worker's complaint writ large across the left rear passenger's door: *MR BORVIS LICKS LITTEL GIRLS*. The drive-in's manager was the only fellow in the county named Borvis. No mistaking who it was. She hightailed it before anyone could catch her.

On the road, she fell in step with the ones who did Renata's Walk. It was a snaky sort of pilgrimage, for there was no direct path. People looped around, through the brush, up and down the highway until they found each other and moved forward en masse, pulsing, murmuring. No one knew the exact point at which Renata Ansky had vanished. All anyone had as guideposts were the crosses, the burned out and relit candles, the sodden lumps of stuffed animals. Marilu passed a gingham rabbit, bright pink, and she saw the beginnings of mold around its ears. She pulled her red hood over her hair, as a disguise, as a modest veil. All she and anyone else knew was that the Walk was finished when you reached the sign, lettered in purple.

She moved among them, going with the flow. This was a new route. More likely, no one knew where they were going. Since the two fellows turned themselves in, more and more out-of-towners turned up, from as far away as El Paso and Brownsville. A few wandered up from Mexico. A few wandered down from Oklahoma. Everyone likes a spectacle; maybe Renata's Walk would get real foreigners one day, the way other shrines did.

The newcomers wore sunglasses and comfortable shoes. They cooled themselves with paper fans and moaned about the heat in between contemplations. They took in the scenery, though it couldn't have been all that different from home. Someone patted her head. An old man offered her a sip of water.

It took Marilu a while to realize that these pilgrims had their own agenda. Their course was not set for the purple-lettered sign, not immediately. The roadside tributes thinned. Soon, there was bare grass instead of moldy rabbits. The old man who had given her water pointed. He said, "That's the house." And the group turned and stared across the highway.

It was not Renata's house, nor Delta's, nor

LaRue's. It was a nice little place, limestone, older than most of the houses that had come up in the last ten years. Apple trees, lots of land all around. Marilu zeroed in on what everyone else was looking at, what they had come for. By the apple trees was something of an excavation. Men from the law came to dig and each day they unearthed a little something: a button, a finger bone, a splinter that could have been an arm or a leg, a tooth. The men from the law sifted sand like prospectors and set aside their finds for labeling. From across the highway, the devotees gasped and gaped. Marilu didn't see what the fuss was about; she'd been waiting, ever so patiently, for a skull, something that might make her hair curl. Fingers and teeth were nothing.

She plopped to the ground, hot, seething, her sweater flapping from its hood draped over her head. She waited for someone to notice, but all eyes were turned to the house. She tugged at the old man's pant leg and huffed when he jerked away. Nothing to do but wander home. All the way, she kicked pebbles into the road and cursed the idiocy of her elders.

Her mood was foul until dinner. She swirled corn and macaroni together on her plate. Her mother asked where she was all day. "I might've needed some help canning tomatoes."

Marilu scraped her fork against the tablecloth.

"I did the Walk."

"Well!" Her mother dabbed at her lips. "In this heat. You ought to be careful next time. Take a canteen with you—"

Father, at the head, overrode Mother with his opinion of Saint Ossana of Mantua's parochial school. Though he was a nonbeliever, he was dead-set on enrolling Marilu next fall. "—I'll say what else I please about the church as an institution. But those people don't let you scrape by with an easy A. The motto at those places is *Read or die*—"

"I saw them dig up LaRue Martin today." Marilu straightened as her parents quieted, turned.

Her mother's eyes shifted, suspicious. Her father scoffed, doused his salad in Thousand Island. He watched her, nonetheless.

Marilu went on, now that she had them. She stretched this silence, reveling in the eyes on her. Even the baby, little Candi, paused in her high chair, fistful of macaroni halfway to her mouth. Marilu picked her words with great precision, as though she were selecting gems. What had that movie said about Saint Bernadette after she died? "She was perfect." This was not the right word. Her audience's confusion made her hot. She held still for a moment until she had it. "She was...in-corrupt."

Her mother blanched. Her father reddened.

The baby slung macaroni to the floor.

Marilu uttered, her voice full of wonder for she had placed herself there, watching the excavation of pristine remains, "…and she smelled clean."

Her mother murmured, in spite of herself, "Like what? What did she smell like?"

"Jasmine," Marilu chirped, "and orange and amber and—" She squeezed her eyes shut, recalling the essences she'd read off the bottle of Youth Dew she'd nicked from the general store. (She'd once drowned her underarms with it in the girls' room at school. Miss Lyles had stopped the grammar lesson to ask if anyone had rotting fruit in their desks.) She couldn't remember the last one and finished with, "—and bergamot." She swallowed. She wiped at a phantom spot of tomato sauce. "That's what it smelled like, at least."

She didn't know what bergamot was. It sounded like a type of sausage.

Anyway, it was guaranteed to break the spell. But her mother's expression heightened from its former astonishment to full-blown zeal. Her father made no further noises of contempt; instead, his brow then creased, his lips then pursed. Candi swept up a blob of salad dressing in each hand and slapped her palms together. No one rose to mop it up.

Collectively, they imagined themselves at the

lip of LaRue Martin's hasty resting place. In it, the girl lay, unmarred, pale, her lips full and lashes long. In death, her beauty had been restored—no, heightened. If life had made her plain, here she became a queen. Her eyes opened, lashes wafting against her cheeks, and the Zamora family swooned at the odors of jasmine and orange and amber and bergamot.

Mother had been waiting for this moment. She had long ago reconciled the idea that she did not have to see it, nor hear it. To witness a miracle secondhand was enough for her. Marilu had already become all the more precious to her; her daughter had seen the two fellows, as everyone was calling them. Her daughter had practically caught them. Mother wrung her napkin. Under her breath, she whispered, "I knew it."

Father let the last of his barriers drop. What had kept him from the Great Beyond was long forgotten. The next afternoon, he would go to Saint Ossana of Mantua and make his first confession in twenty-two years. He felt the Eye on him, once again. He would thank his eldest daughter for it until his last breath.

And Marilu, thief, bully, and tiny charlatan, offered her best simulation of modesty, eyes lowered, smile placid. She took up her fork and finished her macaroni.

LUST OF BODY

Emmett was reading from a book of maritime history. He'd come to an account of George Pollard, Jr., captain of the *Essex*. Time passed, and Emmett found himself scanning the page up and down until the words swam. He gathered just enough to know that Pollard had shot and eaten one of his crew. He relayed this much to Rex Henry in the next cell, who said, "They drew lots. The boy wanted to be sacrificed. It was all done fairly."

Emmett grazed through the rest, and his bowels tightened. He wanted to shout that becoming a meal for cannibals was not meant to be the young sailor's lot in life. But it was all there: The crew had drawn straws. The boy had volunteered. The captain had even offered to take his place. Emmett snapped the book shut, stood, unfolded the clothes that the Ladies' Club had gotten together for him, and the special bottle of bay rum given to him by the guard who brought their meals. "On this day," he'd said, "I thought you ought to have something a little better than Old Spice."

Emmett Anhalt was getting married. Magical John, his bride, waited for him behind the visitors' glass.

His mother and aunts would not be in attendance, though Aunt Jewel had ordered a boutonnière from Andermatt's Enchanted Florist. His mother had written to send her congratulations and to say that, despite Aunt Jennie's sourness, deep down, she wished him well. There was a second envelope for him, a card with a funny little cartoon of a groom choking on his too-tight bow tie. Inside, in that same, up and down script: *Your mother wrote to say you were tying the knot today. Best to both yourself and the lucky girl. Ray.* Very likely, this was all his mother had written of him. Emmett decided that this was for the best.

The trousers hung a bit loose around his waist and he cinched his belt one more notch. His shirt was blue and borrowed, his Indian paintbrush and baby's breath boutonniere new, his shoes old. A justice of the peace would officiate, Mrs. Nimitz from the Ladies' Club would witness. Magical's grandmother was maid of honor. The jailhouse was to have a small reception to follow, with a sheet cake and ham sandwiches and tea. There was nothing else they needed.

He'd asked Rex Henry to stand as his best man. The older man had called through the wall between the cells, "I'll be thinking of you. I don't hold with unions of that kind."

"I want to do right by her," Emmett had said.

Rex Henry did not counter this with anything Emmett had expected. *The child could be anyone's. It's the spotlight she wants, not you. As a jewel of gold in a swine's snout, so is a fair woman without discretion.* Emmett had planned to argue with verses of his own, and he was just opening his mouth to pronounce, *The heart of her husband doth safely trust in her.*

Because he did. If their time together had been greater, he might have gone the whole hog, house, yard, dog. Or perhaps they would do as Magical's ancestors had, live out of a caravan and roam from place to place, answering to no one. Yes, the caravan life would do. In his mind's eye, he routed and rerouted their path from Andermatt County, cutting across the Midwest and into Saskatchewan, then maybe back down along the Pacific Coast. They would have ten children and two dogs, and they would each live to be a hundred-and-fifty.

All of that could have been mine.

It made him want to vomit. And he did, into his tiny sink. Obstinacy made his gut fiery; he wouldn't want Rex Henry at his wedding even if the older man begged. He was about to tell him so when he heard a low, slow voice through the wall, *"Who can find a virtuous woman? For her price is higher than rubies."*

And it took only that to make Emmett love the older man again.

The guard who stood outside Emmett's cell cuffed him before unlocking the door. He chuckled, "Wedding jitters. Always get the steeliest of us. On my big day I got sick on my shoes."

They would be doing a walk like this in a month. But Emmett wouldn't think about that now. He craned his head around to catch Rex Henry's eye through his cell, but he saw nothing. The older man's cot was pressed against the cell's far end, and a low squeak emitted as Rex Henry shifted his weight.

Emmett asked the guard to stop and he called, "Won't you shake my hand?"

Another squeak, a concussive grunt as Rex Henry lifted his feet to lie down. The moment in which Emmett ought to have felt resentful was filled instead with a deep, clutching pity. This man, who walked into Emmett's life as a god, was old.

This man, if he were let to live in the world, would die.

He's going to die, anyway, Emmett's brain pulsed, *and so will I.*

No time for foolishness.

Emmett turned to nod at the guard, and let himself be led by the cuffs into the next room, where his bride waited in a lavender suit pegged out just a little for the life that was to come.

The JP joined their hands, the bride's free and the groom's cuffed, and began. *"Love is patient, love is kind. It is not jealous or boastful; it is not arrogant or rude. It does not insist on its own way…"*

Magical John pinked as she grew closer to becoming Magical Anhalt. Emmett had thought of taking her name, but lacked the courage to bring it up. He envied her glow, what he might have felt if he were to become Emmett John, a new man, Magical's helpmeet. But no. Magical would not have wanted him in any other shape. And Emmett would not have wanted her by any other name, though this was what wives did. He looked to Magical's bouquet, bluebonnets and white carnations. He looked to her grandmother, in her lace aqua two-piece, staring at the yellow jacket that bounced off the corners of the little office, her skin saggy, her face tight. When he met Magical, full in the face, he rejoiced when he saw that she had not transformed into a blanched missus. She was and would always be Magical. Just a different name, was all.

They giggled when the JP sneezed halfway through, "Dearly beloved…"

PRIDE OF LIFE

Rex Henry let his mind go. He lay in the cot, limbs tingling as the blood in him coursed, then slowed. In a little while, he could not feel a thing. He meditated this way more and more now, since taking up residence in the Andermatt County jail. He had not managed to do this in years, not since he was a young man.

He was without memory, without name, without hunger or sentiment or agency. It was not sleep, for Rex Henry never slept. He had reached Paradise in this way, only once. What he knew Paradise to be was what he should have had all along in his earthly life. In Paradise, he had risen up, golden and rippling to adoring faces. Just a sea of people, and everyone had loved him.

And he was going to reach it again. He would prefer to do it himself, but he was old, no denying that.

He let an eye open so that a sliver of the world opened to him. There were no walls. There were no shadows. For a moment, Rex Henry had released himself.

The guard who stood in for this shift whistled. "You all right in there, friend?" He had not seen the older man take a breath; it was imperative that they, the older man and his young fledgling, kept going until the end of next month. No one was sanctioned to end them but God and the state, at the day and the hour they declared. The guard called again, "You napping or what?"

The older man shook, one quick jolt, as though the life had been dropped back into him from a great height. Then he blinked. And he rose, resting his weight on one elbow. He pierced the guard with two black eyes. "I was," he gnarred.

The guard watched as Rex Henry resumed his place in the cot, locked and straight. He did not leave the older man until supper was served, leftover ham sandwiches from the younger man's wedding. On a plate was a gaudy slice of cake, thick chocolate icing, lavender sugar roses. The guard tip-toed to the bars, tapped with his ring finger. The older man slept and drew not a breath.

Before sliding the tray through, the guard popped the biggest rose into his mouth. Perhaps the old fellow would think he got a bare slice when he woke.

BIG BAD WOLF

"Aren't you afraid?" Magical Anhalt asked around a bite of cake.

Emmett held her hand through the slot in the visitors' glass. Now that the words were said, the kisses exchanged, they were back to their respective sides. "Of what? Old Sparky?"

"No, of Cheez Whiz." Magical rolled her eyes, but her nose was red.

Emmett had lots of time to be reasonable about this. He'd asked his attorney to lay out what would happen to him in plain English. And it was all very simple: somewhere in the neighborhood of two-thousand volts, over in five minutes. And after that—nothing. He'd been more keyed up about his polio vaccination.

It all felt deceptively easy.

The girls visited him again early that morning. Renata and Delta and LaRue sat at the foot of the bars and blew what looked like red bubble gum at him. POP POP POP, one after the other. Sometimes, they would orchestrate a rhythm: *shave-and-a-haircut-two-bits*, and once, the *William Tell* overture. The bubbles would break and leave syrupy smears over their mouths. The girls grinned, showing rows of bloodied teeth.

It was hard to tell what Rex Henry made of them, if he saw them. They had not spoken in any real way for days.

Emmett swallowed and picked at a sugar rose. He nodded to Magical's belly. There wasn't much to see as yet. Magical had said that once she began to show, her grandmother would forbid her to leave the house without a coat, even if it were hotter than Hades. And then she would swell. She would split open. "Aren't you afraid?" he asked.

She toyed with the veil on her curvy little hat. She looked as though she might cry. "Of what? Birthing?"

Emmett felt something inside him loosen. "No, the Big Bad Wolf."

And she exploded, a horse laugh that burst

from her chest. She fanned herself with her napkin, then daubed the corners of her eyes. He joined her, and he howled until he could no longer catch his breath. He caught sight of himself in the glass; his eyes were wide, his teeth long, his hair wild. A Big Bad Wolf, indeed.

Magical sniffed and tapped a little rhythm against the faint curve of her belly. She chanted, *"Who's afraid of the big bad wolf, the big bad wolf, the big bad wolf?"*

And they roared again, for it was all they could do.

Beyond the glass, Renata and Delta and LaRue joined hands and danced.

MY BODY

Mrs. Zamora pounded on her oldest daughter's bedroom door. "You're going."

Marilu shrieked, but no amount of volume kept the muffle out of it. She wished she'd kept her mouth shut. Better to live out her days as what she was, the little miscreant, than to play the good girl.

Her mother had made her a white gown with itchy lace around the collar. It made Marilu look like a swollen cupcake. And she was being made to wear it and to sit in it for three hours. There were fates worse than death, and this was one of them.

Saint Ossana of Mantua was becoming a real beacon for pilgrims, these days. Who knew that a little parish in the hills would house one of the great saints to be? That's what everyone was saying, anyway. This morning, the county would gather for a celebration mass in LaRue Martin's honor. Her remains were to be interred in the church walls, behind a portrait of the girl illuminated by real opal and gold leaf.

Father Simon Kavka heard through the altar boys' grapevine that a neighborhood girl had seen the body of LaRue Martin in her shallow grave, head to toe, consummately intact, not a hair out of place. He did not believe it until LaRue herself visited him that night in a dream. She came to him in her postulant's robes, and the whiteness of the veil blinded him. She trailed scents of jasmine and orange and amber. The following day, he went to the place of her burial, in Rex Henry Burr's yard, and was not discouraged when the law gave him splinters and crumbs. He weaved into the crowd that had gathered that day, asked if anyone else had seen LaRue Martin as a whole. All shook their heads. An old man piped up, "There was one little girl. I only saw her the once. She was real quiet. She never came again."

Simon Kavka asked, "You didn't happen to catch her name, did you?"

Another face, a woman, said, "I'm from Andermatt. If it's the same little girl I'm thinking of—" she shook her head, "—I still can't believe it."

The priest persisted, and the woman continued, a little uneasily. "Well, I just can't believe it. I mean, this is the same little girl who made a very indecent gesture at me when I saw her walking home from school one day...I just can't see how something like this would happen to *her*—"

"And she was the only one of you who saw LaRue Martin?"

The woman nodded. "Yes. None of us saw a thing, just dirt. That little girl—her mother's a lovely woman, but that little girl..."

The Apostle Luke had said, *I came not to call the righteous, but sinners to repentance.* Father Kavka did not question the Lord's choice in who would be let to see. There were the last of his doubts, flying away.

LaRue's mother entrusted what was left of her daughter to the church, and the convent at Elam proclaimed the girl as one of their own, a Sister of Adoration. Her consecrated name was Agnes Sabina. That was how her portrait was titled, with her secular name engraved in smaller letters below. In September, Father Kavka would play host to the bishop of the Archdiocese of San Antonio, who would take the first steps toward the girl's canonization.

Meanwhile, Maria Luisa Zamora was becoming a legend herself. Already, a rumor was going around that the bishop had plans to declare her a Servant of God. And her, not even dead!

Her riotousness, her curses, her thieving, went unnoticed, unpunished. Never had she misbehaved more, and never had she felt more impotent. She swiped candy bars from the general store, under the blind, wide-open eyes of Vera at the counter. She smeared chewing gum into JoAnn Sheehan's braid in class. She called Miss Lyles a "fusty cunt" when the teacher tried, feebly, to stop her. She bit Scotty Batista's ear, practically right off—and what do you think his mother did? Not damn thing.

It would be easy to blame her mother for it. Mrs. Zamora was superstitious by nature; if she were not religious, she would still knock on wood, throw salt over her shoulder, anything to keep luck in her favor. Mrs. Zamora had worried for her daughter's soul in confession, and wondered aloud if, now that Marilu had seen the glory, she was now a lightning rod for the devil's mischief. The little girl was touched, there was no doubt.

And everyone was always touching her, laying their hands in Marilu's hair whenever they could. Her mother's friend, Mrs. Glau, spat at her when she passed. "You'll thank me!" the old bat sang. "It keeps Old Scratch away."

Marilu burrowed deeper into her coverlet. She screeched again; her throat burned. She'd used all the ugliest words she knew, and she should have said nothing at all. Another shriek, shuddering, worse than a bobcat.

She hopped from her bed and rolled beneath it. Her mother was threatening to axe the door down. "YOU'RE GOING—"

BREAD OF HEAVEN

Rex Henry and Emmett sat side by side for the first time in months. The older man, who ought not to have been surprised by any change, gave the boy the once over, his eyes widening. Before he could help himself, he said flatly, "Filling out." And he turned away.

Emmett wanted to reach for him, but his hands, like Rex Henry's, were cuffed. So he faced forward.

On the other side of the visitors' glass, four pairs of eyes, all bespectacled, looked back. Emmett could not put together individual faces. He could register what they wore: suits, blue or grey, plain ties with coppery stickpins. These were not lawyers, they were men from the state. They introduced themselves, and Emmett could swear they all had the same name. They explained their functions, but Emmett's head felt full of worms and he could only nod. He let Rex Henry articulate, as he'd always done, for the two of them. Meanwhile, he watched the pattern in the linoleum floor until he saw the patterns: leaves, horses, stars, leaves, horses, stars…

Emmett did manage to catch a few things.

One of the men from the state reminded them that they were to be moved to Huntsville that Saturday. He asked what their plans were for afterward.

Clever, Emmett thought. The man had only said what he needed and let Emmett's brain fill in the blanks.

The man asked again, "Will anyone be claiming either of you? Afterward?"

Here, Emmett inserted his mother, the place in the yard where she buried the old cat they'd had. As much as he'd tried to wedge it, it didn't fit. She'd never mentioned anything and neither had he.

And Magical, too full of sparks, was not one to play the veiled widow. He couldn't ask her to be That Poor Woman. She had said as much, "I'm not going to die with you, you know." He was relieved to hear that, and he blessed her for it: Magical would go on just as she was, not swayed by anyone, man or god.

Another man from the state prompted, "No burial arrangements ?"

Rex Henry told them No.

Emmett told them No.

Rex Henry said, "It's just me and the boy."

Emmett's mouth twitched, but he was in too deep to say anything. He felt Rex Henry's hand upon him, once again. *It's just me and the boy.* It was almost as good as *I love you.* It was, and would always be, just the two of them. He allowed himself to smile, unmindful of the runner that leaked from his nose to his lips. He would go anywhere, if only to touch Rex Henry's hand.

One of the men from the state passed a tissue through the gap in the glass.

Another of the men coughed, peeled off his spectacles. He put his fingers together. "Well, there are options you have…"

One of them stuck out.

The men nodded to Emmett, and one of them addressed Rex Henry. "Is the boy of age?"

Rex Henry confirmed that the boy had turned eighteen.

"Do you or the boy have plans to donate your organs?"

Rex Henry said that they did not.

Another of the men tried to smile. "That's a good thing, actually. The Texas State Anatomical Board is willing to—"

Emmett blinked, and the glory of it caught him. He opened his ears to be sure that he was taking it all in properly. When he confirmed that what he heard was what he thought he'd heard, he let himself lean back against his chair and sigh. It came out in a gush: *"Wow…"* He sounded like Judy Garland, going up for her Oscar. *I'd like to thank all the little people.* If this were truly an award ceremony, Emmett would cast a regal hand to Renata and Delta and LaRue, that bitter trio of wraiths, who seethed in his great audience. He would be bigger even than they were.

This was what would happen. Once it was all over and done with, the state would claim his and Rex Henry's remains and clean them and preserve them. Students would learn from them. People would see them. People would know them. They would come to them from forever, devotees in their own right.

The hugeness of it dizzied Emmett.

Rex Henry, at his side, was less enthused. He kept the same stoniness, hands still atop the counter. Maybe the hugeness of it was too much for him, too. Emmett could hear him breathing.

The men from the state returned the following morning with letters from the Anatomical Board. They were delighted, their letters read. "Thank you for your donation."

Emmett's attorney, a thick little man with a goiter, told the boy to hold his horses. "There's always paperwork, and you always read it," he'd said. And there was paperwork, reams and reams of it. The attorney asked, "Any infectious diseases? Ever had any organs removed, appendix, tonsils? Malignant tumors?"

A doctor had examined Emmett and Rex Henry that morning and marveled at their health. "Sterling," was his word, and then he'd laughed, for he did not seem to know what else to do. "I think we could shower you both in dirt and you'd turn it to gold. I've never treated anyone who couldn't remember the last time he'd taken ill. You make terrible patients." He laughed again.

"Ulcers?" the attorney droned. "Any head trauma?"

Emmett shook his head to all of it. "My first time to a doctor was today. In my whole life."

The attorney winced at the glitter in the boy's voice.

Later, Emmett read aloud to Rex Henry to see if he might perk up the older man. He read of the ossuaries in Czechoslovakia, where the bones of monks were arranged along the walls like sculptures. "They even made a chandelier out of them," Emmett remarked, and tapped the picture, though Rex Henry couldn't see it. It was a tourist attraction, pulling in thousands of visitors from all over. "That's nothing, compared to what we'll have."

A sigh from the next cell. "We're not some sideshow act."

Emmett closed the book. "No. But people will know us. Isn't that why we did what we did? And for the girls?" This last he said with less certainty than he'd hoped. Renata and Delta and LaRue had never seemed at all appreciative. He'd tried to tell them last night how ungrateful they all were. And the thanks he got: hideous shrieks that lasted until sunup.

Rex Henry tried again, "People ought to come to reflect, not to ogle."

Emmett spoke before he thought, and he was too exasperated to care. "What's the difference?" He pointed out all the shrines that Rex Henry had told him of, the Apostle Peter's chains in Rome, Saint Edmund's arm in Connecticut. "What's important is that anyone is coming at all. They can look first, reflect later."

Another sigh, so heavy. "If they wanted to do that, they could just go to Mr. Ripley's Odditorium."

"He has shrunken heads, and so does Rome." It was the first time Emmett had ever talked back to the older man. A low sort of pleasure accompanied it. "Same thing."

He was answered by a bang on the other side of the wall. Was it Rex Henry's fist or his head? It had some give. Emmett rushed to the edge of the bars, but now, as always, he could not make anything out in the next cell.

Then, a low rumble, "We are not a sideshow act."

Emmett nodded, murmured, "I know it."

"You've got other things to think about just now. I doubt you've given your wife a second thought. All the trouble you went to, to do right by her, as you say."

The younger man sunk his teeth into his lower lip and tasted blood. "You never even liked her."

"Doesn't matter. Doesn't matter one fig if I liked her or not. I was under a clear impression that you thought very highly of her. Yes?"

Emmett swallowed. "Am I supposed to like her? What am I supposed to do? You tell me." He knelt and called into the next cell. "You tell me, you're so smart."

"Supposed to—supposed—" Here was Rex Henry, sputtering. Here was Rex Henry, out of his element. "Supposed to—you're not supposed to do anything."

"What?"

"Are you a damned dog? Did I train you to fetch the newspaper, or some such thing? Was that all you were made to do in this life?" Here was Rex Henry, sounding human. "I'll say one thing for that girl of yours. She's full up with filth, but she won't let anything happen to her that she doesn't want to."

Emmett grasped for the Rex Henry from before, who knew all and elevated them beyond the masses. "She doesn't believe in us." He didn't actually know if this was true; he'd never talked with Magical about what all he and Rex Henry had done.

She'd worn his pea coat on a hot day. The look in her eyes when she touched it. How Emmett had told her to take it off. How it put him at sixes and sevens to look at her looking at him.

It was not far from how Renata and Delta and LaRue looked at him on the nights when he could not sleep. They were no longer the ones who saw to see. They might as well have been nothing more than a single, fleshy pile, joined by their common regressions of what it meant to use the senses they had left to them. They had forgotten pity and forgiveness, for they had no use for it. They stank. They oozed. They howled. As rejectamenta, what else would you do?

"No." Emmett could hear Rex Henry's bones creak through the wall as the older man eased himself to the floor. It was the closest they'd been in a long time. "She believes in her." Rex Henry sniffed and went on. His voice had loosened, almost slurred, like the beginnings of drunkenness. "She's full up with filth, and still they come to her. I bet you didn't know that, did you? All those blemishes, the little lepress. Full up with other men's disease. It's a wonder it didn't touch you. Still. It doesn't seem to put anyone off. It didn't put you off."

The older man laughed, the sound oily. Emmett had never heard him laugh, and he didn't like it. "She could sway the masses, if she put her mind to it. She'll be a bigger god than you or I ever will. Disease. Infection." Rex Henry stopped. His voice rose up again in a wandering hum, and he enunciated a few of the words, *Hay-lo, everybody, Hay-lo.* The sloppiness of it struck the air with a chill. Again, he laughed. "But maybe that's good for you and me. Maybe she'll tell about us. Apostles are salespeople. Salespeople are whores. People don't buy shampoo, they buy the fellow who sings that little song—" Again, he sang, *Hay-lo, everybody, Hay-lo.*

Emmett tried to imagine this man in the next cell, great and craggy and omnipotent, but that voice pushed a cartoon in his place. The boy waited for an anvil to fall and shut him up. Emmett couldn't conceive of him in such an undignified position as sitting on a floor.

He called to the guard on watch, who had been pretending not to listen. "Have you given him anything? Has he been drinking?"

The guard shuffled to the edge of the cell next door, peered in. "Doesn't look to me like it."

"It sounds like it," Emmett snapped.

"He looks unwell, if anything. Upset, you know, in his mind." The guard stepped back into view. "And I can't say that surprises me."

Then Rex Henry's voice, heavy, "I'm tired."

"You'll get supper in a minute," the guard said. "A little sedative with it, like you been getting. That'll make you sleep good."

Rex Henry echoed, "I'm tired." The last syllable dripped. "I'm tired."

"Well, it's Swiss steak night, tonight." The guard turned away, mumbling, "Aren't you lucky?" He bent to sniff into Emmett's cell. "Goddamn, young man. How often they let you shower in this joint?"

The odors rose so thickly that Emmett could no longer smell them. He sat in his own stink until they led him to the big bathroom at the end of the hall. It was green-tiled and had frosted glass in the windows.

"And what day they come to get you hosed off?"

Emmett shrugged. "Don't know." The days and weeks melted together, even now.

"Well, let's make it today, hey? I was ready to complain about an old dead rat down here somewhere. Turns out it's you, young man." The guard shook his head. He faded away and up the stairs, and Emmett caught the last of his rumbling, "Call that *dignity for the damned*, 'cuz I don't. No, Lord, I do not."

The guard returned with trays of Swiss steak and a knobby pink towel for Emmett. "Get all that down and we'll get that stench off you."

The Swiss steak and Emmett's underarms wound together in their smell. Summer was coming and, despite the presence of electric fans, the basement cells collected the heat. Emmett sweated. He did not know how much more from himself he could strip until he found some comfort. Before, one hundred degrees, ten degrees had all been the same to him. If now he was to take a bite of his hand as he did the Swiss steak, would he feel the sting?

He ate what he could of the meat and scraped the gravy aside. He filled himself with the carrots, the slice of cake that looked leftover from his wedding.

In her small house, across the table from her grandmother, he saw Magical having her own supper. She ate and ate. Her grandmother had a garden and they fed on onion pies and squash casseroles, stuffed peppers and tomato salads with rosemary, blackberry cobblers. The baby would come out with sprouts for hair.

Emmett thought, I do like her. I like her an awful lot.

"You get your medicine down yet?" The guard poked through the bars with a nubby finger. "Don't forget. I'm to make sure you take it, young man, and you don't pull any tricks."

And the boy rose. With graceful movements, like a magician demonstrating his act step by step, he bent, plucking the little blue pill from its place on the tray, right on the intersection between the meat and the cake. He made a flourish, moving the pill from one hand to the other. Was it in his left hand? No. His right? Why, no—and here it was, in his hip pocket. Into his mouth it went with a big gulp.

The guard slapped his hands together. "Well, now! A real Houdini we got here!" He cuffed the boy and led him along the hall by the elbow. "I used to have a handle on that trick, myself. I could pull a nickel out of your ear, if I had one on me."

Emmett stopped himself from saying, "That's okay." He wedged the little blue pill so that it lay cradled in the flat place behind his bottom row of teeth. In the shower, he would wait until the air was full of soapy fog to spit it out.

TAKE, EAT

Rex Henry listened to himself. The words
bounced off the walls and burst, feeble as bubbles.
"I'm tired," he moaned. "I'm tired. I'm tired."

Emmett, like all inmates of their kind, had to
be watched in the shower. Strings of Head and
Shoulders crept into the hall, carrying little bits
of the guard's voice over the water. No one had
come to replace him; it would only be for twenty
minutes, tops.

There was no one there to hear the older man.

He hadn't touched his supper. For a while, he
sat and watched the gravy gelatinize over the meat.
A yellow jacket banged between the bars before
settling atop the slice of cake, nibbling at the sugar

rose. When it was done with that, it moved to the carrots for whatever sweetness they had.

Rex Henry wedged himself into the space between his cot and cabinet. This was where he kept the books from the Ladies' Club that wouldn't fit anywhere else. He spun around on his rear and sat before them, as though he were trying to decide what to read before bed. He ticked his finger against the spines. *Northanger Abbey. Sense and Sensibility. The High Window. Tamerlane and Other Poems.* He pulled this last from the middle of the stack, a hardback book that held ten of the thirty little blue pills he'd been given with his evening tray. The rest he'd swallowed down, beginning at half-past three that afternoon.

That was the way to go about it. All in moderation. One at a time.

His head was coming away from his shoulders and the feeling was marvelous. Things went bright, then dark, bright, then dark, like a lighthouse's whirring beam. He took one, perused these words that could not keep still, *From mine own home, with beings that have been / Of mine own thought—what more could I have seen?* He laughed. He drooled, and the letters oozed over the page. He took another. He slurped at the thin stream from the faucet. Then another. Another.

Steps in the hall. A new guard, a young man,

apple-cheeked and stringy. He took his place in the folding chair set outside Rex Henry's cell. The young fellow barely looked sixteen.

The older man hailed him with rippling fingers. "Hey there." He proceeded to pull his trousers down over his hips, and let his sex dangle, wormy from the root. It didn't matter what he did now. He was not a god. He announced his failure to the young guard, "I made a hash of it. I really did."

The younger man tried to look away. His cheeks were now the color of plums.

"I say, I made a hash of it. You hear that?" The older man sank into the column of books. He spread his arms wide as they collapsed over him. "I'm tired," he whimpered from under them. There was no glory. This was it. "I'm tired—"

In a minute, his fingers twitched.

In another, he was still.

MY BLOOD

The guard was not hugging Emmett so much as keeping him in one place. The towel had fallen. It was luck that the guard had his arm pinned over the boy's hip, so that he was not completely exposed.

The cell had been emptied of the older man in record time. Rex Henry might have ascended without Emmett, and this was what he wanted to believe. Taken, body and soul, like a true martyr. But he could smell the older man's refuse from his last moments. They hadn't time to clean that up yet, nor the blood from when Rex Henry had fallen forward and scraped his chin.

Saints did not make ugly smells.

His chest felt opened, and something reached in and squeezed.

Emmett wriggled in and out of the towel and shrieked into the empty hole, again and again. "YOU SHIT—"

THE EVERLASTING COVENANT

Rex Henry Burr was born in San Francisco in 1906.

Rex Henry Burr was born in Chicago in 1885.

Rex Henry Burr was born in Europe in 1914, on the very day Archduke Franz Ferdinand was shot.

Born in time for an earthquake, a plague, a war to end all wars.

Rex Henry Burr was a mortician.

He was a hitman for the Mob.

He was a retired Marine.

He never married.

He married three times, twice divorced, once widowed.

He had no children, other than the boy.

He had a child, born to a woman of low class, somewhere in Himmel Creek, very likely that Mongoloid girl seen hanging around the porch at the dance hall.

He kept children in his basement.

He kept mummified hands.

He had a pet orangutan.

He had a pet boa constrictor.

He had a pet wolf.

When all of this filtered into the county jail, from lips to ears to lips to ears, Emmett roused his brain long enough to think, *Well, they got that part right. He did have a dog.*

Mrs. Nimitz had said that Mrs. Glau had said that she'd known Rex Henry for as long as she'd lived in Andermatt, and that was most of her life. Mrs. Glau was eighty-five.

The guard from the first shift said that the guard from the second shift said that the guard from the third shift had said that Rex Henry had peeked into his sister's window one night as she was getting out of the bath. "Is that true?" the guard from the first shift asked.

Father Simon Kavka, who now came daily, said that he had never seen Rex Henry at his services.

"We went to one," Emmett told him. "And we took confession. The both of us."

"Really?" The priest sat back, as though he might get a clearer picture of the boy the farther he craned his head. "I thought I would've remembered." His eyes widened. "What did you say? I would've thought I—"

Emmett tried to recreate the scene. These walls were of knotty cedar, and this space much smaller. This was the confessional, outside were the naves. Saint Ossana of Mantua had a high, pink ceiling, painted with golden stars, and the air was close and murky. He could nearly smell the incense. He repeated what he'd said that day, word for word: "I am in love."

The priest nodded. "Yes."

Emmett blinked, back in his cell and too heavy to lift his head. "That was it. I am in love."

"With whom? Last I heard, love was never anything to be—"

"I did things to get it."

Simon Kavka rolled his palms together. He'd heard many meditations on the subject of love, and it was not unusual to hear of a man's willingness to jump from a bridge for it. But he was not yet ready to look at love's underbelly. Jumping from a bridge had a romance to it. So did martyrdom. He let his eyes slide from the boy's eyes to the boy's hands. The fingers were long, the nails packed with grime. They called to mind the gangly knuckles of an ape. To Simon Kavka, the boy sat in that disquieting place between man and beast. He moved slowly, should anything set this creature off.

Then, with great precision, and (this made Simon Kavka shiver) in the pinched scholar's tone of his mentor, Emmett recited a passage from the Song of Solomon: *"His left hand is under my head, and his right hand doth embrace me."*

And in that instant, Simon Kavka imagined himself beneath that pink vaulting, dotted with stars. Saint Ossana's eyes were blind and blank; someone had scrawled a moustache beneath her nose in thick pen. The stars came unstuck and dropped from the ceiling, like cheap children's décor. Something had shifted, and the tack of it, the glitz, and the little girl in the red-hooded sweater who now dotted a big mole on the statue's cheek, the absolution that would come so she could paint the Virgin's lips in red and return for more forgiveness, the thick perfume in the air, the words that never stayed in one place.

And now this creature.

Six months after the boy's execution, Simon

Kavka would turn in his collar. He meditated and found, for the first time, that he was mostly talking to himself. In another month, he would send letters to Rome. In one of them he wrote, "The relief of having nothing there is preferable. I don't believe that I could continue, knowing that my love and yearning is not only unrequited, but perhaps also manipulated. All I ask is to be let go, very quickly." In another year, his laicization was made official. In another year, he took up a position in the Phillip D. Andermatt Library, and lived out his days with an ease he had never known.

FRUIT OF THE VINE

The State Anatomical Board of Texas will not accept donations under the following conditions:

If the body has experienced decay.

If the body has harbored disease of any kind.

If the body has harbored malignant growth of any kind.

If the body expired under trauma, such as a car wreck, gunshot wounds, or suicide.

Emmett asked the men from the state, "What will you do with him?"

The men from the state glanced from one another before continuing. Since Rex Henry Burr hadn't any burial plans, the state had taken matters into their own hands and had the remains laid to rest in the old fever cemetery in Himmel Creek.

"Not here?" Emmett asked.

Not here, the men from the state told him.

"Can I see him?"

Again, the men from the state were made to look at one another. Since Rex Henry Burr had no next of kin—no next of *blood* kin, they added—the county thought it best to have the remains cremated. The ashes had been scattered again, since Burr hadn't made burial arrangements, the county felt that a headstone was unnecessary.

Emmett munched at this. Everything came to him in slow waves; he felt this was a good thing, as it was better to see destruction's approach from miles away. It didn't hurt so much.

But here was a fact that came too fast to see: Emmett Anhalt would be alone. Tomorrow he would go to Huntsville. The day after, he would be wheeled away to Baylor University, emptied, pumped up, pickled and pilloried for the world to see, once the scientists were done with him. He'd already signed the papers. The attorney had okayed them. Magical had put her signature down as a witness and his next of kin. Nothing to do but let it happen.

He had lots of time to think. Already, he felt

his faculties begin their shutting-down and he hung suspended in a pleasant haze in which he felt nothing at all. He could not read, though Mrs. Nimitz from the Ladies' Club promised to bring him anything he liked. ("Anything within reason." And she'd tried to smile.) He spent the time watching the patterns in the ceiling change: starfish, birds, petals, circles, and dogs, running and running until his eyes went fuzzy.

Renata and Delta and LaRue sat behind the bars. They were nice to him this time, patience cooling them until they looked nearly as they had in life. They still could not speak, but they could play games. Emmett tried to remind them of Hangman's rules. On a piece of notebook paper, he sketched the scaffold and beneath it five lines. It took a little longer, for LaRue was the only one of them who could recall her letters. They passed the paper and pencil stub back and forth through the bars. Renata and Delta scrawled lines and shapes mostly, sometimes something more coherent, a flower, a swollen heart. LaRue seemed to be slowing down, too. Her script was blocky, but legible, though her mind wandered, like someone about to nod off.

"Come on," Emmett coaxed. "You know this one. It's just one more letter."

LaRue made a line.

Emmett nodded. "Okay. You're almost there. It's the only one you haven't guessed."

LaRue's jaw sagged, freeing a runner of spittle from her lips. Her companions had collapsed into one another, heads together, erupting in loud, fitful snores.

"Come on."

LaRue made another line. Emmett took the paper from her and held it in the overhead light. R O Y A L. The little stick man had hanged long ago, but she'd gotten it. He gave her the thumbs up. And, as though he had granted her permission, LaRue yawned and sank away into eternal slumber.

Emmett wept.

GOLGOTHA

"God," Magical said through the visitors' glass. "This is a real spread."

And it was. Emmett and Rex Henry had put in their requests for their last meals a month in advance. They each had a budget of fifteen dollars, very generous of the county. Perhaps this was a peace offering, one that said, *We'll take your life, but we won't let you go without a good supper.* And now that Rex Henry had gone, Emmett had inherited the older man's final privilege.

Thirty dollars purchased a true feast: Chili and biscuits and succotash and roast chicken and scalloped potatoes and French toast and onion rings and ketchup and pickles and Spanish rice and kolaches stuffed with lemon curd and blackberry pie and vanilla ice cream and bottles of Big Red, courtesy of Dear Liza's Café.

Magical started on the French toast. "Wow."

Emmett bit into a pickle, then a chicken leg. His appetite was hearty. He'd heard of inmates ordering lavish meals and refusing the plates when they were served. The guard on this morning's shift told him of a man who had shot his wife for insurance money. Before he was hanged, the fellow had ordered a full Thanksgiving dinner, turkey, stuffing, yams. "And when we brought it to him, he puked right into his salad bowl. He didn't have the stomach for it, of course. Then the fellow said, *Why don't you all dig in, seeing as I can't touch it, myself. Don't let it get cold.* Now, this was two days after the real Thanksgiving, so the jailhouse boys, prisoners and guards and all, all got to have a second turkey dinner."

He recounted the story for Magical, who was scraping syrup from her plate. "That's sweet of him," she said. She didn't look weepy or pale. She looked as though this were another day, and Emmett was off to see the wizard, instead of to Huntsville. Why was she so pink and robust? She'd been taking out the seams of her skirts in the past couple of weeks, and something below the waist did look a bit swollen. Today, the pleats in her dress fanned about it. Would a baby keep a girl this buoyed, no matter what? Was that all she needed?

Emmett took a sip of Big Red, licked the pink from his lips. He leaned forward. He asked her to promise him something. "Just this one thing."

Magical nodded, her eyes bright. Emmett thought she looked almost blank behind her pinkness. "Whatever you want." That was it: She looked as she had when she visited wearing his heavy pea coat, numb to that day's cloying heat.

"You need to listen," Emmett went on. "It's serious business."

Magical nodded again, her head practically bouncing. Where was her sharpness, her way of looking at every angle from the corner of her eye?

Nevertheless, he had to keep going. He swallowed. "You know where I'm going tomorrow. After everything's over with."

"I do."

"You signed the papers. I guess you also read them."

"Sure did." This he believed.

"A lot of people are going to be looking at me."

Magical beamed. It made Emmett shiver. "I know."

"Now, look." He tried to put an edge to his

343

voice, as Rex Henry had done. "I'm serious. So, here it is. If anybody asked who I am, why I'm there, what I did to get there." He swallowed again. "I don't want you saying anything. If anyone asks about Emmett Anhalt, just say, *Who?*"

Magical's face gathered to the center. She folded her arms, the hands steepled atop her belly. "Just say, *Who?*"

"That's right. Just say, *Who?*"

The divide between them was thin, cold. Emmett continued to hold her hand through the gap in the glass, but his was limp, despite her constant squeezing. Was this what Rex Henry had wanted, devotees who would do nothing more than sit and blink at them through this barrier, like things in a zoo? Already, Magical, his wife in name and everywhere else, was petting him. To her, he was already gone, gold-plated and preserved and pretty. Perhaps she would not survive the great flood, after all.

But then she smirked. He could feel her edges again. He tried once more. "You promise me you won't say anything?"

Magical shrugged. "About *who?*" And she winked, and resumed her pink idiocy, for the guards had come, at last.

They clapped a hand on Emmett's shoulder and waited for his wrists to be cuffed. "You ready?"

COMPLINE

Somehow, the dress had gotten more hideous than the last time she'd worn it. If before she had looked like a cupcake, she better resembled now a three-tiered wedding cake. Marilu slammed the screen door behind her, plopped onto the porch steps. Her mother had forbidden her from sitting anywhere that was not already polished and scoured, for the dress was white Galway lace. "From Granny Maureen's wedding dress," Mother had added. She'd added layers to the skirt and taffeta wreaths to the sleeves. And the veil was from her other grandmother, her Abuelita, who kissed her and prayed over her when she arrived last night from Monterey.

Marilu was to receive her first Communion. That part alone would have been all right, but everyone had it all planned out. Her parents had petitioned and her grandmother had argued for Marilu to be the one to carry the relic of Saint Agnes Sabina in the Communicants' procession. Agnes Sabina wasn't the girl's real name, but Marilu couldn't remember it. The girl was not yet canonized and everyone, even the Protestants, even the nonbelievers, were referring to her by her consecrated title. Then, the family would pile into the car and they would make the four-hour drive to Baylor University. They had tickets to see Emmett Anhalt, his full form on display at the College of Medicine.

"You need to see for yourself," her father had said, the one who had, until now, always been on her side.

It made Marilu sick.

She sat, picking at the mosquito bites around her ankles, daubing at them with the underside of her lacy socks. A spotty pattern bled through. The porch was crusted in a layer of pollen. Marilu imagined getting up just before her mother came to the door, exhibiting the yellow-brown stain over the Galway lace. Maybe this would be enough to keep her home, or at least pump some temper back into her parents. All this time, they'd been going around, their faces frozen in high, holy smiles. Any more of this, and Marilu feared her head would turn to mush.

She rubbed the veil's hem over the step, satisfied by the brown streaks.

A far away barking lured her to the edge of the front yard. Thanks to the dress's added layers, Marilu waddled through the grass, the train picking up twigs and acorn shells. She climbed the fence and leaned over its pickets. The barking shallowed to happy panting, though it seemed to have grown louder, closer. And there, crunch-crunching through the bramble across the road, was a dog. A funny-looking thing, body like a sausage, short legs, coat like a melted chocolate sundae.

"Hey," Marilu called. "Hey, puppy dog."

The dog trotted to her outstretched fingertips, sniffed them, licked them.

Marilu busied herself with the animal, kisses, nuzzles, pets, and when she next looked up, it was to a pregnant lady in a lavender dress. "This your dog?" she asked.

The lady came to the fence, slow, taking care to balance herself, according to the burden of her belly. "Not mine. We have kitties at home." She scratched under the dog's ear. "You know what? I think I've seen this pooch around. Isn't this the one that's always getting out and chasing goats?"

Marilu shrugged. "I dunno."

"I like the getup," the lady said, making a figure-eight at the little girl with her fingers. "You getting married, or something?"

"No." And Marilu told her some about what it meant to make your First Communion.

"You got all dolled up to eat crackers?"

"And we get to drink wine." Marilu tried to make it sound glamorous, even if it was only going to be a sip.

"You excited?"

"No."

"Then, why get dolled up?"

"So everyone can see me...and my ma said."

The lady nodded, ran a hand through her short black hair. "I know how mas do. And grandmas."

Marilu sighed. It was as though, for the first time since the beginning of all this, someone could hear her over the static. Too, Marilu felt herself standing a little straighter, trying a swagger to her voice. You could do and say such a lot without doing and saying very much. She leaned against the fence, hoping she looked as hard-boiled as she thought.

The lady perked an eyebrow; Marilu couldn't

read the humor in it.

"And then," the little girl went on, rolling her eyes hugely, "we're going to go see a dead body."

"Yeah?" The lady seemed too cool to be interested. Perhaps she'd already heard enough about it.

It wasn't enough to quiet the little girl. Not quite. "Yeah." And she shook her head. She repeated what all she knew of the body, plus how he had died. "Five thousand volts, they killed him with. They had to shave his head first, so his hair wouldn't catch fire."

The lady nodded. "Yikes."

"Yeah. And I'm going to see him."

"You sound excited." And the lady sounded stiff.

"I dunno." This much was true. If it were anything else, a Ripley exhibit, the cholera mummies in Mexico, Marilu would have begged to see them. And her mother would have said, "How grotesque! There are better things you could be doing with your time." Marilu kicked at the fence with the toe of her white patent shoe. "I just wish I didn't have to look like a snowball to get to see them." And the idea that she was being made to see them was like an itch beneath her tongue.

The lady patted the dog's rump. She straightened, her hand splayed over her watermelon belly.

She looked as though she might go, but she rocked on her heels, and she bent to tuck a lock of hair behind the little girl's ear. "How about we go for a stroll? Just around the block. And when we get back, maybe you'll figure out if you want to go or not. Just around the block."

Marilu peeked over her shoulder. In the house, her mother was still ironing the good dresses. Her father, cutting into his eggs at the kitchen table, had not yet showered. Abuelita was bathing Candi. And there were always lost keys, misplaced gloves, a thousand little mishaps that seem to happen on Red Letter days. There would be plenty of time for a stroll.

Marilu took the lady's hand and they set off. The dog followed.